BUT GENTLY DAY

BUT GENTLY DAY

ROBERT NATHAN

1 9 4 5

ALFRED A KNOPF

NEW YORK

For STEPHEN VINCENT BENÉT —

*from whom I have so
often borrowed beauty, and pride, and courage*

BUT GENTLY DAY

CHAPTER ONE

Eᴀʀʟʏ on a stormy morning in November,
1942, a farmer in the lamplighted kitchen of his
home near Landons, outside of Millersville, heard
a plane in the air above him, traveling north toward Hemlock Mountain. The November storms
had been unusually severe that year; the plane was
low, from the sound of it, and laboring; outside, it
was still pitch black with night, and the wind was
blowing strong. It's a bad morning, he thought, and
hesitated before going out to water his stock. A
few minutes later, while he was still hesitating in
his kitchen, he heard the loud but distant smack of
an explosion, and almost at once noticed a red glow
in the sky in the direction of Bitter's Ravine. "I
didn't figure it would be anything I'd care to see,"

he explained later, "but I got my boots on, and went over.

"It was a powerful hot fire," he added, "but the woods were wet. I'd be just as happy not to remember any of it."

As the grey dawn gathered in the sky, the wreckage of the plane lay on the mountainside, on the black, burned-over earth. The hot, twisted metal cooled slowly in the cold, rough wind; while the sheriff and his men beat at the smoking ground, and searched the charred bodies for some token of identity.

))§(())§((

THE SUN was not yet up; a mile away, down the slope, the mists of autumn lay motionless in the hollows. It looked as though it would be a fine day. The road ran east and west through the pass; a narrow path cut down across it, flanked by an old stone wall, on which two men had stopped to rest and talk.

Corporal Arkbester was on his way home; he had a ten days' furlough in his pocket, and he was anxious to see his family again, and the girl he expected to marry. His companion was an older man; Corporal Arkbester had met him a little earlier, farther up on the mountain. He had never seen him before, but he was respectful of his rank which was that of a captain and a chaplain in the United States Army.

Corporal Arkbester had not been surprised at their meeting on a lonely forest path so early in the morning. He knew just where he was: he figured himself to be about two miles from his home in Randal's Meadows, and three miles east of Landons by the Millersville road. It was part of the respect that he felt for a superior officer, that it did not occur to him to ask the chaplain where he was going.

As they sat together on the damp stones, talking and resting, the sun rose up over the trees. At once, shadows sprang out across the ground, and their eyes filled with yellow light; trees and rocks stood out bright and clear, washed yellow in the air which was fresh and cold as spring water. Far off in the west, the last faint shadow of night melted in the sky.

The chaplain leaned backward, his fingers laced about his knee. "You were saying," he declared, "that you could not see what would happen when the war was over. I admit, it is difficult, unless we view what we see through the eyes of faith. In that case, it is permissible to hope, I think."

"What I think is," said Corporal Arkbester, "there's too much bad feeling in the world. I don't see how anyone's going to forgive his enemies, after what they've been doing."

"The human mind is resilient," said the chaplain. "And besides, there is no choice."

"That's what stops me," said Corporal Arkbester; "people being like they are; but if you can't get along with them, what happens to the world?"

"You ask me something I cannot answer," replied the chaplain, "except to say that after many disasters, man and the world are both still here. I admit that man has not lived as long as the crab, or the virus; but he has made more improvements in himself."

"Well," said Corporal Arkbester, "he's got himself into a mess of trouble this time."

"Perhaps he has," agreed the chaplain soberly; "perhaps he has. However," he added, "let me ask you a question"; and leaning forward, he gazed at the young man earnestly: "Do you believe in God?"

Corporal Arkbester felt uncomfortable, for he did not like to be asked such a question. "Well, sir," he said politely, "I'm not what you'd call religious-minded, if that's what you mean."

The chaplain settled back again with a sigh. "So many are not these days," he said. "It is a pity, since you lose the comfort of it. But in that case, let me ask you something else: are you not afraid to die?"

Corporal Arkbester reflected, for he wanted to give an honest answer. At the same time, he felt a lump in his throat, because of the beauty of the morning, and because he had only ten days to spend at home. "I guess we're all afraid to die, sir," he said, "when we stop to think of it."

"When we stop to think of it," said the chaplain slowly; and nodded his head. "Yes," he said, "that is it. It is strange; because in the end, there it is, and we have not taken the time to prepare ourselves." And he added thoughtfully,

"What do you think it is like, Corporal?"

"To die, sir?" asked Corporal Arkbester.

"Yes; to die."

"I don't know," said the corporal uncomfortably.

"Have you ever wondered about it?"

"Yes, sir," said Corporal Arkbester. "Often."

"Well, then," said the chaplain; "tell me; what do you think it will be like?"

Corporal Arkbester was silent for a moment. Then he said slowly: "I read in a book once, that the brain goes on dreaming for a little while . . . afterwards."

"Indeed," said the chaplain. He seemed to be thinking it over, but he did not commit himself. "It is an interesting idea," he said at last. "I do not know whether I quite like it."

"I don't think I like it at all, sir," Corporal Arkbester admitted.

"'To sleep,'" quoted the chaplain to himself; "'to dream.' Of course," he added, "it might be a good dream."

"It might," agreed Corporal Arkbester, "or it might not. Anyway, it's the last one, and you don't wake up from it."

He shivered a little in the cold, morning air. "You take it with you," he said. "Whatever it is."

"It would be a comfort," remarked the chaplain, "if you believed in God. For then whatever you took with you would have great meaning."

"Yes, sir," said Corporal Arkbester. "But I don't see what I'd say to Him, or Him to me, and that's a fact. With the world the way it is."

At this, the chaplain smiled. "And what do you know about the world, my friend?" he asked gently.

Corporal Arkbester had the grace to blush. "Not very much, sir," he said humbly. "But I've seen things my grandfather never heard of. I've heard of hate; and I don't like to think of what's ahead, not for winner or loser, either one."

He rose, and stretched himself. The chaplain also rose, and the two men moved a few steps together down the soft, forest path, covered with the brown leaves of autumn. "I haven't very far to go, sir," said Corporal Arkbester. "The road ends down there aways."

"I shall go along with you, Corporal," said the chaplain.

They walked on down the path, over the dead leaves which made no sound. The sun was higher now in the sky, in which the autumn tone predominated, misty and light. All about them was quiet, the quiet of the woods and the soundless air. The light shone brightly on the dark trees, glinting yellow from the bare boughs; and now and then a sudden fragrance made itself noticed, as they passed a spot where the sun had already warmed the earth. A wedge of duck flew overhead, above the trees.

"What sort of people do you come from, Corporal?" asked the chaplain at last.

Corporal Arkbester replied that he came of farming stock; but he felt obliged to admit that his father had sold off most of the land. "He didn't take to farming," he said. "He wanted to be a doctor, but it didn't work out for him."

"Why not?" asked the chaplain.

"Times got bad," said Corporal Arkbester, "and Theodore — that was my grandpa — kept him home to work the farm. Grandpa wasn't a good farmer; he never had his heart in it. My great-grandpa Absalom was the only good farmer we had, in our family. He made it pay. But not Theodore."

When the chaplain asked him if he had ever known his great-grandfather, Corporal Arkbester shook his head. "Old Absalom?" he asked. "No sir, I never did; nor my great-grandma Ivy, neither.

They were very old. They died before the turn of the century."

"And were there any others?"

Corporal Arkbester looked thoughtful. "Others?" he asked. "Well, I don't know . . . I guess so. There was a great-uncle; I sort of forget his name. And a great-aunt Becky, but I always heard she came to a bad end. I never saw any of them."

"Did you ever see your grandfather?" asked the chaplain.

"You mean Theodore? Yes . . . I saw him, I guess. But just barely. They say I take after him in looks. I can't remember Grandma, because she died before I was born. There was some story about them, about their being married; I forget what. She was in love with a soldier, or something. Though there's a funny thing."

"Yes?" said the chaplain.

"Why," said Corporal Arkbester, "her name was Eileen." He reached into his tunic, and drawing a square leather portfolio from an inner pocket, passed it over to the chaplain to look at. It contained a somewhat faded photograph of a young girl, across the bottom of which was written in a delicate hand, "To Henry with all my love, Eileen."

"I do not suppose," said the chaplain, "that this is your grandmother?"

The young soldier smiled shyly. "No sir," he said. "It's surely not."

"Your wife, perhaps?"

He shook his head. "No," he said more slowly, "not exactly. Not yet. We sort of thought we'd wait to see what was left of me after the war."

A last light feather of mist drifted between them. In the forest silence, he tucked the portfolio back into his pocket again. "It didn't seem like a good idea to get married," he said, "not knowing would I ever come home again. But I think maybe we were wrong."

"Do you?" asked the chaplain quietly.

Corporal Arkbester shivered suddenly. "We've got our own lives to live," he said; "haven't we?"

The chaplain made an almost unnoticeable gesture of restraint. "I have never been altogether sure," he said.

The woods were thinning out around them now, and the path on which they found themselves was more clearly marked. Beyond a rise, hidden by the trees, they could see a narrow plume of smoke in the air, as though from a distant chimney; while along the way, at short intervals, were ranged large piles of logs cut and split for firewood. Corporal Arkbester stopped, and looked at them in surprise.

"Now who'd be cutting wood hereabouts?" he said.

"Your father, perhaps?" said the chaplain. But Corporal Arkbester shook his head.

"Father never split a log of wood in his life," he declared.

"And besides," he added, "these logs are hickory; and there's been no hickory around here since I can remember."

Proceeding down the path, they passed a rocky clearing in which a small herd of cows was grazing, their bells musical in the bright morning air. "This was all our land once," said Corporal Arkbester. "The folks we sold it to didn't aim to farm it, so far as I know."

A little while later, rounding a bend of trees, they came out onto a rising sweep of meadow, in the middle of which, between two great trees bare of leaves, stood a square farm house of grey and sober stone. Corporal Arkbester caught his breath. "Yes, sir," he said; "there she is. That's my home."

But as they started up the meadow toward the house his steps faltered, and finally stopped altogether. He stood looking at the house as though he were uncertain about something. "There's something funny here," he said. "They've done something funny."

He held his hand up against the sun, in order to see better. "They've taken the porch off," he said slowly; "the one that Grandpa built. Now why would they want to do a thing like that?"

He shook his head, and looked at the chaplain with surprise. "The barn's been shingled over, too," he said. "They didn't tell me."

"Well," he said; and took a long breath. "Will you come in with me, sir?" he asked. "I know my folks would be glad to make your acquaintance."

"Thank you," said the chaplain. "I think I will."

Side by side, the two men ascended the long slope of meadow to the house.

CHAPTER TWO

THE WOMAN in the kitchen was small and dark, and though no longer young, gave an impression of being birdlike and delicate. She was dressed in woolen cloth, and whoever else she was, she was not Henry's mother. When she spoke, she cocked her head a little to one side, like a sparrow. "Come in, young man," she said. "I don't know who you are, but you look familiar. And you too, sir," she added politely, noticing the chaplain's cross. "Mr. Arkbester is et and gone," she said.

They stepped into the warm, bright kitchen, with its good smell, not only of bread and baking, but of the old house itself, of wood and plaster, of peeling paint and faded wall-paper. She stood in front of them, her small hands on her hips, and looked them up and down. "You," she said to Henry, "are an Arkbester, or I miss my guess. I thought I knew them all, but I expect I was wrong."

Henry looked around him with simple joy. Here he was home again, he thought, and it smelled just the way he remembered. That was the thing about home, even though it didn't always look the same, it never smelled any different. It didn't look quite the same now, he realized; what with that big iron stove over there against the wall . . . that was new; his folks had had a gas stove ever since he could remember. And so were those pots along the shelf new — there, where his mother used to keep her cans of fruit and vegetables. "Isn't my mother here, ma'am?" he asked.

"I purely doubt it," said the woman; "or if she is, she forgot to tell me. Who is your mother, young man?"

"Why," said Henry in surprise, "she's Mrs. Arkbester. I'm Henry.

"I've been in the army," he explained. "I've just come home."

The woman studied him for a while, her head on one side. "Henry," she said finally; "well, now, I don't know. It seems as though I ought to recollect you, Henry, but I don't." She smiled with a sort of sour amiability. "It doesn't matter," she said. "If your mother's coming, she's coming, and you may as well set and wait for her."

"That's just what I figure to do, ma'am," said Henry politely. And he thought to himself, Now whoever is this?

A frosty light shone for a moment in the woman's eye. "Do you indeed?" she said. "Well, now, that's forward of you." But as she looked at him, standing there surprised and innocent, she softened, and added not unkindly, "You come from afar?"

"Yes ma'am," said Henry. "I've been traveling all night; and some time before that."

She had the pleased look of a woman who knows what is needed. "Are you hungry?" she asked. "I wouldn't be surprised."

"That's right," said Henry. "We haven't et yet."

"Well," she said, "there's tea left over hot in the kettle. And if you'd care to freshen yourselves first . . ." she pointed to a rough door leading out of the room, "the basin's there."

"That's the woodshed," said Henry.

"So it is," she agreed. And she added coolly, "What's the matter with it?"

Nothing, thought Henry; it was queer, that was all, to be told to wash up in a woodshed. Why not go up to his room, as he always had? It was there, wasn't it? or had they maybe changed his room since he was away? He didn't remember any wash-basin in the woodshed.

Still, it didn't seem to matter very much. Probably they'd used his room for something else. He didn't feel like arguing about it; he felt more like going off to the woodshed, as he had been told. I guess I'm used to taking orders, he thought.

In the shed, the light was dim, and the air was fragrant with chips of cedar, spruce, and hickory. The wooden wash-stand in the corner was furnished with a white china basin and pitcher, and a rough hand towel; Henry and the chaplain plunged their faces into the icy water, puffed and shivered, and rubbed themselves dry on the rough linen. "I sort of had my mind set on a nice hot bath," said Henry. "We never had a wash-basin set out here before."

He slicked back his hair, peering at himself in the small mirror which hung above the wash-stand. "They've certainly done things over," he declared. "They've certainly done some funny things." He looked at the chaplain with sudden doubt. "You don't think they could have sold the place," he asked, "without their telling me?"

"I shouldn't think so," said the chaplain.

"This lady," said Henry uncertainly; "she said I looked familiar. But I never saw her before."

"Perhaps she is a relative of some sort," said the chaplain.

"She could be a cousin," admitted Henry; "I wouldn't know." He fingered the light stubble on his chin. "I dislike to shave in cold water," he said. "If I had to shave in cold water every day, I'd sooner grow a beard."

He glanced around him at the walls with their piled logs, at the dusty window through which the sun sent a mild and pallid beam. "This shed," he said, "with the light in it; it's like when I was a child."

"It is an early morning light," said the chaplain.

"When you were young, it was always like that."

"That's right," said Henry. "It seemed like it was always morning."

Freshly washed, they returned to the kitchen, where a breakfast of fried hominy, tea, and apple pie awaited them. But although Henry sat down with a good appetite, he found himself most of the time watching the woman, who stood looking out of the window, one hand on her hip, a long wooden spoon in the other, and her lips pursed in thought. She was not unfriendly, but he had to admit that she had an air of belonging there; she didn't give the impression of being a stranger, or of being in any kitchen but her own.

He wasn't sure just when he began to think that something was wrong. But after a while, he found himself wondering why this woman, this stranger, should be standing there in his mother's kitchen as though she owned it. A stranger, and still no stranger from her talk, if what she said was true . . . knowing the family, that is, but not knowing his mother, and not knowing him. What was she to his father? He wanted to find out.

He began, by asking with a casual air,

"Didn't Pa know I was coming home?"

"I can't say either as how he did," she replied, "or didn't."

"Didn't he speak of me at all?" asked Henry, surprised. It was hard to believe that his father wouldn't have said something. Unless, of course, he hadn't received the letter that Henry had sent him.

"Didn't he speak of you to whom?" asked the woman patiently.

"To you," said Henry.

"I don't know as how your pa ever spoke a word to me in his life," she said flatly, "or I to him. What's more, I wouldn't know him if I was to see him."

It was a relief to Henry at first — until he realized that it left him back where he'd started from. Puzzled, he looked across at the chaplain, as though to ask him what to do next. "Perhaps," said the chaplain, "this lady can tell us when Mr. Arkbester will return."

She turned her quiet gaze back to the window again. "He went over to Landons," she declared, "to see Cyrus Craik about the loan of a team. He shouldn't be too long . . . unless they get to talking."

Yes, Henry thought, that was like his father, always one to be late for whatever he was doing. But Cyrus Craik was a stranger to him; and the woman had said that she didn't know his father.

Wasn't his father Mr. Arkbester? Or, if not — who was he, then?

He glanced around him at the kitchen, familiar and — now that he looked at it more carefully — unfamiliar, too. It was not alone that the iron stove, with its ornamental knobs and curlicues, made the whole room appear more substantial; it seemed to him that even the pots looked heavier than he remembered. Among them, iron predominated, with now and then the orange gleam of copper; over in the corner, where there used to be a broom closet, he now saw a great wooden barrel, for flour from the looks of it; and bags and sacks were lined up along the shelves of the cupboard where there had once stood painted canisters of tin, and toasted cereals in paper packages. The white porcelain sink was gone; in its place was a great pan of zinc, set in a heavy frame of wood, scrubbed clean, and lemon-colored in the sun.

Corporal Arkbester took it all in, slowly and soberly. That something was wrong, that something had happened here, was more and more apparent; but as to what it might be, he had as yet no idea. Out of the corner of his eye, he studied the woman; a line or two in the way she stood, an angle in the poise of her head, cocked a little to one side, reminded him of someone, awoke the echo of a memory in him . . . from far away, from long ago. What was it his father used to say? Don't be like . . . don't be like whom? He couldn't remember; it had to do with being stubborn, he thought, and having your own way, and making other people pay for it.

Certainly at first glance she didn't seem to be stubborn; not till you looked at her twice, and saw the thin set of her mouth, and her eyes, which for all they seemed dark and gentle, could wrinkle suddenly at the corners and turn not merry, but sharp and cold. Her woolen dress, high-necked and heavy, hung to the floor, and swept it when she walked; she had a narrow waist, and her shoes were low-heeled, but buttoned high.

It was the shoes he looked at longest. Now wait a minute, he thought; now wait. People haven't worn shoes like that, not for a long time.

He glanced across the table at the chaplain, to see if he had noticed anything. But the chaplain was sitting with his hands folded peacefully before him, and with a calm and patient look on his face. It was a strong face, Henry noticed, but gentle, too; and it reassured him.

He looked once more around at the full shelves, at the food piled on his plate in front of him; and he cleared his throat. "You folks eat pretty well," he said, mustering up a hearty manner. "I'm glad of that. I'd sort of heard we ate better in the army than they did at home."

"Is that so?" said the woman. "Well, it's news to me." Her mouth set in a sudden, bitter line. "Don't talk to me about the army," she cried. "We had our fill of it. Four mortal years of war . . .

"Maybe we've made a little cash money," she said more quietly; "but it didn't come easy. What we have, we've worked for; and no thanks to any but ourselves."

"Yes, ma'am," said Henry unhappily. "I didn't mean it that way."

She sighed, and put the spoon down on the table. "Well," she said wearily, "finish your breakfast. There's a lot to do in this house, and I've got to get on with my work."

She turned to go, but paused suddenly, arrested; and moving swiftly to the kitchen door, pulled it open, and peered out across the cold, brown, sun-glittering earth. "I thought I heard something," she said.

Shading her eyes under her hand, she stood looking; and then she nodded her head. "There's the team," she announced, "just coming over Beecher's brook. I'd say he'd hardly took but time to go and come. Cyrus must have clear out-talked him."

A dog barked, far off, racing toward them; Henry could hear him coming up the meadow toward the house. She stood in the doorway, waiting, looking out, her face lighted and eager, with the sun making a thin gold rim around her hair. He could hear the crunch of wheels outside, the jingle of harness, the clop, clop of horses. "Now, then," someone cried; "you, Theodore . . . take hold here."

Henry sat very still. That's not my pa, he thought; but he was not surprised. It was as though he had known all along that somehow or other it wouldn't be his father. Someone else belonged here, belonged with the woman with the high-buttoned shoes, and the iron stove and the big flour barrel. It was like a puzzle, with the parts just ready to be put together; soon, in a minute or two, it would all be clear. And still, all the time, there was the feeling of being among his own people. It was a good feeling. He knew where he was, he wasn't lost, or among strangers; he was home.

Swift, light feet sounded on the gravel, mounted the kitchen steps. A thin, wiry man, bearded, gray, dressed in homespun, and followed by a youth of twenty, came in through the door. "Well, Ivy," he said; "we got visitors?"

"We have," she said, "though I don't know is it family or what. Maybe you can figure it out, Absalom."

And turning to Henry, she nodded her head.

"This is Mr. Arkbester, young man," she said.

CHAPTER THREE

Henry and Theodore sat side by side on the wooden fence of the pig-pen, and watched the three large sows and the dozen or more smaller pigs tramping about in the sour mud. The young men were of about the same age, and they seemed to have no trouble getting along together. "Not," said Theodore, "that we haven't plenty of other kin folks that we don't know about. Though I guess," he added shyly, "I like you about as well as any."

He pointed to the insignia on Henry's sleeve. "What's that for?" he asked.

"That's the Army Air Force," said Henry.

"You don't say," remarked Theodore. "Well, what next?"

He fidgeted a little on the fence. "There's a lot of

new things in the world," he announced. "There's a lot of things I'd like to see." And he added with a sigh, "Sometimes I wish I could get myself more education."

"Well," said Henry, "why not?"

"I don't know," said Theodore uncertainly. "I expect Pa needs me here. Though I do feel unrestful, now and then."

His eyes, ranging the horizon of bare, November trees, took on a dreamy look. "I read the other day," he said, "that there's more than three hundred and fifty young men studying at Princeton University, over in New Jersey."

"No," said Henry; "that isn't right." He frowned at the ground, trying to remember what was wrong with it. "I don't think it's right," he said.

"I thought maybe it was too many," said Theodore meekly. "Another thing," he went on; "about California. They say the land is running with milk and honey. Have you ever heard that, Henry?"

"I've been there," said Henry slowly.

"You have?" exclaimed Theodore. "Well . . . is it like they say?"

"No," said Henry.

Theodore nodded his head. "That's what I feared," he said.

He was an earnest young man; he longed for better things, at the same time that he was resigned to their being beyond his reach. What he wanted most of all, was to improve himself; he would have liked to improve himself materially, as well as morally and spiritually, but it seemed unlikely, though not impossible. "After all," he said to Henry, "I guess you can find cause to be satisfied wherever you are, if you live upright, and do your duty.

"I am not without ambition," he added shyly.

Ambition . . . duty . . . they were two equal words in Theodore's head. To stay — or to go; both equally teased him, but to stay was simpler in the end; and it asked less of him.

"Most things are best left the way they are, I guess," he said.

But he could not altogether give up the new, the shiny world. "I've never seen much," he said humbly. "I've never seen Niagara Falls, or even Philadelphia." He sighed a little. "I'd like to see one of those new marble wash-stands," he declared, "like they have now."

"They won't last long," said Henry.

"Well," said Theodore doubtfully, "I don't know. They sound like they had great advantages in winter."

It was peaceful out there, behind the old barn, in the sun. The pigs made a low, muddy sound at their feet; and Henry could hear the creak of a pump, and the wooden clatter of a pail, as Absalom drew water. It is a fact, he thought, that morning here is different, in light and sound, from what I remember. It seemed to him that the sun lay more freshly on the earth, and that the air was clearer and quieter; he experienced a feeling of innocence, and exclaimed,

"This is the way it must have been."

Absalom, who was passing at that moment, stopped by the fence, to give the pigs their water. "I don't know how it used to be," he answered. "My pa settled here before I was born. I was born right there, in the house."

Yes, thought Henry. And so was I. And more, that you never heard of.

Absalom continued: "We used to take our wagons into Lancaster, a good three days each way. Now we've got three railroads clear across the state. I don't know but what it's going to change things considerable."

"Some day," said Theodore boldly, "we'll travel all the way to Ohio on a steam railroad."

"I purely doubt it," said Absalom. "What's more, I wouldn't care to do it. My father lived his whole life in this county, except for the once he went to Philadelphia. I disremember he ever thought he was improved by it. Travel is most likely to fill the world with strangers; and then, by God, we'll have another war."

"Now, Pa," said Theodore, "you know you find it easier to get to market."

"Well, so I do," said Absalom. "But how far that adds up to a solid advantage, I'm not prepared to say.

"Though I do aim," he admitted, "to get myself one of these new-fangled steam threshers, or else a feed cutter from Vermont. A man needs machine help these days, what with the kind of hired labor we're getting." He spat, suddenly and bitterly.

"That's what the steam cars have done," he said. "Coming and going, coming and going . . . carrying the young men away."

"Clear beyond Pittsburgh," said Theodore.

"What good can come of it?" asked Absalom.

He ran his hand across his lips, under the wiry stubble of his beard. "Up and down," he said, "across the land. Bringing us the world's troubles, Ku Kluxers and carpet-baggers. By God, you tell me which is worse."

"Ku Kluxers are worse," declared Theodore; "they are violent men."

But Absalom shook his head doubtfully. "There's a bitter feeling over all this country," he said, "like a blight; and it's going to take more than steam trains to cure it. What we done to the South, they'll hold against us till Kingdom Come.

"You mark my words."

This is the light and the sun, thought Henry, of long ago; seventy years ago, or eighty. It looks real, too.

The trouble was, it felt real. It would have been easier if it had felt like dreaming . . . but it didn't feel like dreaming. Because in a dream, only part of the dreamer is there; he leaves most of himself asleep, only his eyes look out at things. They look out into a half-world, in which nothing has ever happened until he dreams it. But this world where Henry was, was real; and all of him was there in it. Nothing was left behind, no part of him was left sleeping. All that there was of him, was there.

And Absalom, and Theodore — they were there, too, true and solid and satisfied; they had been there before, and they would be there afterwards. Supposing he were to say, "I can tell you what the world will be like long after you are dead" . . . They wouldn't have known what he was talking about. They were too solidly rooted in their own time and place; they saw what they saw, and they knew what they knew. He was Cousin Henry to them; they thought that his parents' names sounded familiar, though they couldn't place them. Whatever he might have said, they would have turned it into something homely. Running hot and cold water? They had it in Harrisburg.

And anyway — could he have told them what it would be like tomorrow and the day after? Not any more. For Henry himself had begun to forget; it was as if certain things were no longer of any use to him, and so were beginning to fade from his mind, into a kind of distance . . . into guess and wonder. Or sometimes only a part of something forgotten . . . remembering how it felt to fly, for instance, remembering the lonely peace of the sky — but not why men flew, or on what errands. "Flying?" said Absalom vaguely; "well, yes; I do believe there's been some experimenting around."

It was queer, the things he had forgotten. Where had he gone to school — and what were the names of his teachers? And who was President of the United States? He tried to recall some fact from the past, to see what he could remember . . . What had they had here, behind the barn, where the pigs were now? He didn't know. Not pigs; flowers perhaps? He couldn't remember.

After a while, it didn't matter. He guessed there had always been the pigs there. They seemed the most reasonable things to be.

The chaplain was up at the house, talking to Ivy; and Henry went to find him. "Were you going on, sir?" he asked. "I'd like to say good-by."

"I was," said the chaplain, "but I am in no hurry.

Unless Mrs. Arkbester would like to be rid of me."

"No indeed," said Ivy. "I'd be pleased to have you visit here awhile." She was still in her kitchen, seated now on a straight-backed, wooden rocking chair, friendly but no less respectable. Her hair, neatly coiled on top of her head, was not yet gray. "We don't have very much company," she said. "Or social doings."

She was not complaining; and she didn't mean to be. Company was rare, that was all, and social doings were limited: there was the County Fair, threshing suppers, and church sociables, and she had been to Harrisburg once to see the play *East Lynne*, at Fulton Hall. It was not that her life was lonely, for she was much too busy to be lonely; but distances were great, and people lived at home. Besides, there was more to her family than they had seen; she had two younger children at day school in the valley — Becky, aged fourteen, and John, aged twelve. There had been another boy after Theodore, but he'd died of inflammation of the bowels, at an early age.

"The children don't get home from school till late afternoon," she said. "I don't know if I hold with so

much education. For John, maybe; but for Becky
. . . a girl ought to have had enough school teach-
ing by the time she's twelve. After that, she can
learn what there is to learn in the kitchen, and be a
help to her mother.

"Like I was, to mine," she said.

The chaplain looked at her gently. "Perhaps your
daughter wants to see more of the world," he sug-
gested.

She shrugged her shoulders impatiently. "She'll
see no more of it," she answered, "for wanting to.
A woman sees what's put before her. She sees her
husband's home, house and land, cattle and children; she sees her rain barrel for soap, and her flour
barrel for bread. She sees her spices and her herbs,
her woolens and her linens. They'll mean forever
more to her than marble halls; and that's as it
should be.

"As you, a minister, should know," she added.

"I do know," said the chaplain. "And yet, the
human heart has room in it for everything."

"All a woman needs in her heart," said Ivy, "is
piety. The rest she can leave to the men.

"Well, no," she added after a moment's pause.

"She'd better have purity too, for both of them."

"I was wondering about that," said the chaplain. "I thought perhaps you had forgotten."

"No," she said. "I didn't forget."

There was, Henry thought, something indomitable about her; but something bleak, as well. She had made up her mind about the world, and she had taken up the only weapons within her reach. Purity and piety . . . what an old-fashioned armory, but how sufficient. She was like a fort in the wilderness.

"Henry," she said, "do you know, was Mr. Arkbester aiming to fill my lard bucket for me at the store today?"

"No ma'am," said Henry. "He didn't say."

"Well, you go find him," she said, "and you ask him. And tell your cousin Theodore while you're about it that if he's planning to go down in the valley today, he can fix it so he'll meet Becky and John on the way from school, and bring them home with him. That Becky can just give me a hand with the supper tonight."

Henry went out again on his errand. He found Absalom and Theodore in the cool shadowy doorway of the great barn, examining an Oliver chilled plow in which a speck of yellow rust had appeared. "She wants her lard bucket filled," he said.

Absalom reached into his hip pocket, and pulled out a plug of brown Pennsylvania tobacco. He looked at it thoughtfully; and then he put it back again. "You aiming to go anywheres special?" he asked Theodore.

It seemed to Henry that Theodore's face grew a little rosier. "Well," he said uncertainly, "I thought maybe you'd want me to go back to see about that team some more."

Absalom nodded. "You might, at that," he said; "though you're not fooling me any. You stop on down to the store, and fill your ma's bucket for her. Seven cents a pound, it is. I don't know why to God she couldn't wait till we'd had a chance to try out some of our own."

"She said to tell you to bring the children home from school," Henry said, "if you could fix it."

"Well, then," Theodore declared, "I'll do it after dinner. You want to come along, Henry? I'll stop at the store; and I'll stop at Mr. Craik's house; and then I'll get the children."

"Don't you stop too long at Craik's," said Absalom. He gave Henry a bright, sly wink. "You see to it he gets on with what he's got to do, Henry," he said. "And you see he gets home again.

"And what's more," he added, with another wink, "if you happen to meet up with a certain young lady on the way, that won't surprise me any."

CHAPTER FOUR

From the high seat of the light farm wagon, Henry looked down at the broad, brown back of the mare, the great, patient muscles pulling between the shafts, the long tail swishing across the reins. The mare ran with a sort of coquettish movement of her haunches which soon became stained with little ripples of white and yellow foam. The wagon smelled of leather and old felt, of sun-baked wood, axle grease, and apples; and the warm odor of the horse came back to him on the breeze. This is nice, Henry thought. It was restful to take so much time to do things.

The cold air and the bright sun made patterns on his face; and he looked curiously around him at the countryside which he knew, but which was no longer altogether familiar. He realized that this was because it looked the way it used to look when he was a boy. The world around him had grown smaller, while the distances within that world, from hill to hill and tree to tree, had grown larger. From a wagon seat, the horizon seemed very close; but beyond it stretched a country of infinite size and unknown wonders. In that world, Ohio was a strangeness and a distance, not something to fly across in an hour, faster than a bird. It would take a long while to get there, even by rail.

Theodore was in a happy mood; he seemed to be stirred by some inner excitement, and to be enjoying a secret of his own. As they drove along, he pointed out places of interest to Henry, some of which Henry knew, and others which were strange to him. He knew the road down which they were going, but the trees and farms were more abundant than he remembered; he saw houses and barns where there had been only waste fields and stony walls, and tall trees where he remembered thickets. They passed other wagons on the road, driven by bearded men dressed in jackets of heavy cloth or corduroy, with high-breasted vests of dark or bright-colored wool. They greeted Theodore gravely, with manly pride.

In Millersville, Henry missed the familiar landmarks; instead of the business block with its drug store and soda fountain, its real estate office, fire station, and motion picture theater, he saw a few old, wooden buildings, an attorney's office, the hall of the new Patrons of Husbandry, the Millersville National Bank, and the Millersville General Store and Post Office, E. Simon, Prop. It was here that Theodore stopped, and drawing up beside a small, roofed-over peddler's wagon on which was painted in flowing script the name A. Neuberger, hitched the mare to a post before the steps.

"Here we are," he said. "Bring the bucket with you."

The interior of the General Store was dim, and fragrant with peppermint, licorice, dried prunes, and spices, and with the mustier odors of poplin and cambric cloth, paper boxes, and trays of notions. A round-bellied stove, not yet lighted, took up the middle of the floor, and beside it stood a wooden box-spittoon filled with sawdust. When the two young men entered, Mr. Simon was leaning back behind the counter, chewing on a wooden toothpick, and listening to Mr. Neuberger who was trying to sell him a length of braiding from a satchel full of novelties and notions which he had open before him. "You will see," Mr. Neuberger was saying; "there will never be a chance like this again. Look at this braiding; just feel it; French, from France. It's special from before the war; they don't even make it any more.

"The ladies will positively go crazy for something like this," he said.

"Excuse me a minute," remarked Mr. Simon, and leaning across the counter, he called out to Theodore, "What can I do for you, Teddy?"

Theodore handed him the lard bucket. "I'll take ten pounds of salt," he said, "if you've got it. And," he added, turning a little pink, "I may find it handy to stop off at Mr. Craik's house, on account of having to pick up Becky and John on their way from school; so if there are any letters for over there, I could probably just as easily take them along with me."

"There's some magazines for Craiks," said Mr. Simon. "*Harper's Weekly,* and *The Country Gentle-*

man. And your ma's *Christian Instructor* is come. I'll go see are there any letters for you."

Left to himself, Mr. Neuberger approached Henry with a friendly but humble smile. "You couldn't use a pair of spectacles?" he asked. "Direct from England."

Henry shook his head. "No," he said.

"Or a fine lead pencil, made of handsome cedar wood, with the best soft lead inside that would make a pleasure of any kind of writing?"

"No," said Henry.

Mr. Neuberger sighed. He was a young man, a little older than Theodore, with handsome dark eyes, and a blue, clean-shaven chin. He looked discouraged, but he did not mean to give up. "A pair of patent leather shoes," he asked, "made in Salem, Massachusetts?"

Henry smiled at him sympathetically. "Times are bad, aren't they," he said.

Mr. Neuberger nodded his head. "They are bad," he admitted, "but they are not so bad as all that. I am not really discouraged; I have great faith in the future. I think . . . do you know what I think?"

He dropped his voice to a whisper. "Some day we will be a very rich country."

"I guess we will," said Henry.

"It will take a little longer," said Mr. Neuberger, "because we have Mr. Grant instead of Mr. Greeley. But just the same, the railroads are going to change everything."

"That's right," said Henry. "They are."

"You agree with me?" asked Mr. Neuberger eagerly. "I am delighted. Do you know that it is possible to go all the way across the country in a steam train, except for a few changes? The possibilities are enormous. Perhaps you would be interested in something." He reached down into his satchel, and brought out a handful of papers. "I have here the stock of a new railroad," he said. "It is to go all the way across Kansas, 469 miles, from Atchison to Dodge City, with a branch besides from Newton to Wichita."

"That must be the Santa Fe," said Henry.

"You know about it?" asked Mr. Neuberger in surprise.

"It's a good road," said Henry.

Mr. Neuberger's face lengthened, and he regarded Henry with sudden doubt. "It is only just built," he said. "So how is it such a good road?"

"I know about it," said Henry.

Mr. Neuberger put the stock back into his satchel again. "Maybe I will keep it a little longer," he said.

Theodore had finished at the counter; now, with the lard bucket in one hand, and the letters and magazines in the other, he started for the door. "Take the salt, Henry," he said. "We've got to go round by the other side of the valley, and leave some things."

But as they climbed into the wagon, he became suddenly silent and reserved; and as they drove slowly along, up the other slope of the valley, the silence deepened. It suited Henry very well, for the cold air and the gentle motion of the wagon made him feel drowsy, and in any case, he had nothing to say. The afternoon sun slanted yellow in his eyes; he let his thoughts drift; and Theodore had to speak twice, before he heard him.

"The Craiks have got their niece visiting them," said Theodore, staring at the whip in his hand, as though wondering what to do with it.

He seemed happier for having spoken, but it meant nothing to Henry. "I remember there was a place called Craik's Creek," he said slowly. But then he wondered, did he remember it, or not? It was across the valley from us, he thought.

"There's a brook on this place," said Theodore, "but I never heard it called anything."

The horse plodded on, and they were silent again; Theodore thinking about Mrs. Craik's niece, and Henry about the far-off autumns of his childhood, spent in the woods around Millersville and Landons, by Craik's Creek . . . was that its name? . . . or up among the pines of Bitter's Ravine, on Hemlock. Yes, he thought, it must have been. It was here, that childhood; and yet it was somewhere else, far away.

The wagon turned into a rutted land, and a few moments later they drew up before a decent house of painted clapboard, with a low porch built along the front. "You wait here, Henry," said Theodore, scrambling down; "I won't be long."

Henry sat on the wagon seat, looking out over the bare fields and leafless trees of Craik's farm. A few chickens clucked in the gravel beneath him, and on a neighboring slope he could see five cows standing, silent and patient in the silvery, autumn grass. The sun, low in the south, made long shadows across the earth, and a flock of rooks settled, creaking and cawing, in the dark branches of a pine. Their harsh cries died away, leaving a stillness bright as light and clear as water.

The girl came into the stillness from around the corner of the house, a light shawl over her shoulders, a bonnet swinging in her hand, a red ribbon twisted in her hair, and the laces of her small slippers crossed above her ankles, under her starched, white petticoats. She stopped and stared, and Henry stared back at her. All around them was silence; only their eyes gazed at each other, full of doubt and wonder.

"Oh," she said faintly, at last.

It can be like that, dreaming or waking. The shape of a face, the glance of entreaty, the smile withdrawn or given; these are for us. They go to our hearts, although we do not know why. The question is never asked, the answer never given; yet question and answer tremble together in the air.

He did not know who she was, but he knew that he had always known her. "Hello," he said.

Confused, she looked down at the bonnet in her hand, as though she thought she ought to put it on. "I didn't expect to meet anybody," she said. "I thought that Theo . . . Theodore . . . was inside, with my uncle, Mr. Craik."

"Yes," said Henry; "so he is."

She looked up at him with a little puzzled frown. "Who are you?" she asked. "Are you a friend of his?"

"I'm kin of his," said Henry. "I'm Henry Arkbester."

"Oh," she said again; and held out her hand. He bent far down from the seat to reach it. "I'm pleased to meet you, Mr. Arkbester," she said. And she added with a pout, which he thought enchanting,

"I don't think it was very good manners of Theo to leave you out here all alone in the air."

"If he hadn't," said Henry simply, "we wouldn't have met."

She looked up at him in surprise; and then she smiled. "You're quite a card, I'm afraid," she said.

But she dropped her eyes under his steady look,

and her cheeks turned a little pink. "You mustn't look at me like that," she said, frowning.

"Well, why not?" he asked. But he looked away, nevertheless. The only trouble was, he still saw her; he could have closed his eyes, and seen her just as plain.

"I don't know," she said. "It makes me feel strange." And she added, with her eyes on the ground,

"It makes me feel as though I knew you."

He wished she'd look up, but she kept her head bent away from him. "It makes me feel the same way," he said. "Only I like it." Yet his voice trembled a little.

Her bonnet took all her attention; she gathered the ribbons, looped them into a bow, and then undid them again. "Are you going to be here for long . . . Mr. Arkbester?" she asked at last.

Henry looked off across the shadowy fields. Was he there for long? He wasn't sure; he had forgotten. "I hope so," he said. "I hope I can stay."

And then, all at once, it was important to know what she was thinking. He leaned down from the seat. "Do you hope so?" he asked.

She gave him one swift, startled, and unwilling glance; and then hid her face again. "Yes," she said, as though she were surprised at herself; "I . . . guess so."

A flood of happiness enveloped him, followed by a feeling of despair. There seemed to him no reason for either . . . yet both were a natural part of this meeting. He wanted to sing, and dance; and at the same time he felt very much frightened. There are little curls around her neck, he thought.

"I've got to go now," she said. "Good-by." Not looking at him, her eyes still hidden, she turned to go. But before she could reach the house, Theodore came out of it. "Well," he cried when he saw her; "where have you been? I was searching all over."

If Henry confused her, Theodore, at any rate, did not. She stopped, the bonnet dangling from her hand, and looked at him with wide open eyes. "Why," she said, "you had all that business with Uncle Cyrus. That's so dull for me, Theo. I thought I'd wait outside."

And she added, like an obedient child:

"Did you miss me?"

She doesn't really care, thought Henry; it's only

something she says to smooth things over.

Theodore was not comforted, however. "After all," he said unhappily, "I only came to see you. And now I've wasted so much time . . ."

He seemed about to weep with vexation. His glance came to rest on Henry, sitting quietly on the wagon seat above him. "Did you two get to meet?" he asked suspiciously.

Her eyes, amused and secret, flashed Henry a warning, or an appeal. Then she looked down again. "No," she said demurely. "Should we have?"

"Well," said Theodore, without much enthusiasm, "I don't know. Anyway, as long as you're here . . . that's my cousin Henry. He's stopping with us for a spell."

"Yes," she said coolly. "Go on."

He turned to her miserably; he was half jealous, and half proud. He touched her shyly on the arm.

"This is Eileen, Henry," he said.

CHAPTER FIVE

I‍т was Henry's turn to be silent on the way home, while Theodore, on the contrary, now that the ice of his secret was broken, wanted to talk. What he wanted to say was far from simple, for in one breath he longed to be told that the young lady was beautiful and above him, and in the next, that he had nothing to worry about. He wanted Henry to praise her, but not to desire her for himself, except in an humble, never-to-be-hoped-for way.

"What I admire about her," he said, "is that she is very educated. She likes to read; and she has traveled as far as Wheeling, West Virginia. It was from her I heard about the marble wash-basins.

"I prefer a woman to be modest, and womanly," he said. "I wish that Becky were more like her."

Henry scarcely heard him. He kept thinking of the young girl they had just left, whose sweet, serious face, and slender, rounded figure had taken complete possession of his mind. He saw her, standing beside the wagon, her head bent, and the brown hair piled high upon it; and what Theodore had to say about her did not seem to apply to her at all. He might as well have been talking about someone else.

For the young girl that Henry saw, was not Theodore's friend, but his. She was no stranger, he knew her well; it was almost as though he had known her longer than anyone else in the world. It seemed to him that he knew things about her that Theodore would never know. He was not jealous of Theodore; he thought it possible to ignore him.

Nor was there anything, any more, in his own life to disturb him. Somewhere, he remembered, there was a girl whom he had wanted to marry; but that had been far away, or long ago . . . And this was altogether different. There was something here beyond doubt or chance; it had always been here, it was as much a part of him as his own flesh and blood. He did not say, I am in love with her; he simply thought, We belong to each other.

His silence took no account of the trip home, nor of the two children who tumbled into the wagon from the roadside in the blue, November dusk. They stood up, behind him, in the body of the wagon, a small boy and a taller girl, swaying as the wheels jounced along over the road, clutching their school books, shy and untalkative. He heard Theodore speak to them, and he heard their replies, but all from far away. It was a mood in which the twilight also played a part, shadowy and mysterious; and in which the frosty peace of the countryside, and his own lonely delight, met together in harmony.

It was not until the family was gathered at supper, that he really saw the children. They sat across from him on the other side of the table with its red cloth, on which the oil lamp made pools of yellow light, and studied him with swift, sly glances. The boy seemed like an ordinary youngster; but the girl, he thought, was noticeably over-grown. She wore a simple, tight dress, in which, as she helped her mother at the stove, her ripe, round body moved with an almost painful fullness; and the expression on her face was mainly one of curiosity and dissatisfaction. He saw the chaplain watching her; and it seemed to him that the chaplain's face, as he looked at her, was full of concern.

"Maybe the minister would care to say grace," said Ivy.

The chaplain bowed his head; and the others followed suit. "Upon this family," he said, "upon Thy children on the heavy road of their life, look Thou in kindness, Lord, and in compassion. Be Thou also here, at the breaking of bread. Thy will be done. Amen."

Ivy and Absalom looked at the chaplain in surprise, and then at each other. "Now," said Absalom; "now." He cleared his throat, and stared uncomfortably at the bowl of soup in front of him. "Hm," he remarked.

But presently, dipping his corn bread into the soup, he gazed around the table with a more cheerful air. "Well, Cousin Henry," he observed, "I hear you've been to Craik's Farm. I hope that Theodore here took proper care of you. I wouldn't rightly have sent him on an errand today, except there was need of it."

He turned to his wife. "Cyrus aims to drive a bargain with me," he said. "He says he'll bring his team over, if you'll give Emma the loan of your sewing machine."

Ivy's lips made a straight, thin line. "I don't know as I can do that at all," she said. "I was expecting to do my sewing, soon as I got the poplin from the store. I'd sort of set my mind on a polonaise for Becky."

"Oh Ma," cried Becky. "Did you really?"

"Why not?" asked Ivy. "You're almost a young lady, and it's time you had a dress. You're grown out of your last-year's woolen."

"A polonaise," breathed Becky. "Oh my. What is it, Ma?"

"I don't know," said Ivy. "There's a picture of it in my *Christian Instructor*. It says . . . wait, now; let me look. . . . It says, 'When unbuttoned it falls into a beautifully shaped Wrapper without pleat or gather. It is also used for waterproof or ladies' cloth.'"

"What does Becky want a wrapper for, Ma?" asked John. "Is she going to get married?"

"Eat your supper," said Ivy. "And don't be indelicate. You mind your affairs, and we'll mind ours."

"Becky is young yet," said Absalom quietly. "Time enough to rig the girl out in fancy clothes when she's done her schooling."

"Well, anyway," said John doggedly; "Becky knows a man."

The eyes of her family turned on her in surprise; and Becky's face grew frightened. "I don't, either," she said.

"You do, too," insisted John. "You were talking to him after school, on the way home, when we passed Simon's Store."

"What's this, my girl?" asked Absalom.

"It's nothing, Pa," said Becky. "It was just that peddler from up north, and all he said was it was a nice day, and I said it was, and that was all it was, and that nasty little boy acted like I . . . like I'd . . ."

Her eyes filled with tears, and she hung her head. "You see," said John, "I was right."

"You be quiet," said Ivy fiercely. "I'm sure Becky's too pure-minded to do wrong by word or deed. All she did, was out of the kindness of her heart."

"Maybe so," said Absalom gravely; "maybe so. Just the same, I don't hold with young ladies exchanging views with the men they meet on the roads. This country is full of vagrants and trespassers; they're like a blight upon us. He may be an honest man, or he may not. If he was, he wouldn't go around speaking to defenseless young girls."

"Maybe he's a murderer," said John hopefully.

Becky gave a moan; and buried her face in her hands. "Now, then," said Absalom; "no need to carry on. Next time he speaks to you, you just go by, and say nothing."

"He's a Ku Klux Klanner," said John.

"That's enough," said Absalom. "I don't want to hear any more about it." And turning to Henry, he remarked,

"It was a hot summer, and a windy fall. Good for the corn."

"I remember there was a wind," said Henry.

Absalom nodded absently. In his mind, he had already started out on the things that bothered him. There were the night-riders in the South, shooting and murdering whites and blacks alike. There was the Pattenburg massacre in New Jersey, where eighty Negro cabins had been burned to the ground. "By God," he said, "where's the dignity of it? My hogs got better manners to each other than that."

He spoke of the bitterness of the South, and the uneasy harshness of the North. "Right here we're in the middle of it," he said. "You can smell the trouble in the air; you can taste the bitter taste of it, do you face either way. I declare, it sickens me; and I don't see the future for it, whatever. Half the country is full of violence, and the other half has got new-fangled ideas."

"After every war," said the chaplain, "the defeated side has found itself at the mercy of desperate and wretched men. They are like children who have been hurt; they are bound to hurt others in return. There is no such thing as victory, except over yourself."

Absalom looked somberly down at the table, and stroked his beard with rough and calloused hands. "It's a trick of the Dis-unionists," he said, "this bitterness between the North and the South. I lay it to the Democratic Party: they've made a crack in this country that time will never heal. By God, sometimes I almost think we'd have done better had we let the South secede."

But the chaplain shook his head. "We did what we had to do," he said. "Where we failed, was afterwards."

"That's right," said Absalom; "and what have we got for it? Taxes and tariffs . . . A farmer pays on twenty articles of prime necessity — mind you — forty-seven and a half per cent in gold. That's true figures, from the books. Well, that can't go on."

He looked up at Becky across the table. "What's more," he said, "morals have got worse."

"Speak for yourself, Mr. Arkbester," said Ivy. "There's nothing for us women to be ashamed of."

"Ma," said Becky, "make him stop looking at me like that. I tell you, I haven't done anything."

"Nor will you," said Ivy grimly, "while I'm alive to help it. Now stop your hollering, and give me a hand with these dishes."

Night stood black in the windows, the frosty autumn night lay outside without a sound. For a moment there in the amber-yellow lamplight in which they all seemed fixed, the mystery of time reached out to Henry, and something like the stilly thunder of eternity sounded in his ears. This was his family, these were his own; from this house and these lives he himself had come; made of the same dust and breath, they passed through the world together. And yet, how powerless they were to save or even help each other, each lonely to himself, and filled with fear and longing.

"You, Theodore," said Ivy, coming to a stop for a moment behind her son's chair, "did you see Eileen?"

"Yes, Ma," said Theodore.

"There's a nice girl," said Ivy, to no one in particular. "As pretty and sensible as she can be. She was telling me only the other day about a book she was reading, called *Little Women,* by Louisa May Alcott. She brought me over a recipe for family Indian loaf."

To this, Theodore replied only with a confused smile. Becky, however, turned from the stove, a wooden ladle in her hand, and her eyes bright. "I wish I could read *Little Women,*" she said.

"Well," said Ivy, "maybe you can."

"How can I," cried Becky, "when I never have

any time?" And she added with a burst of longing,
"I wish I could be educated and refined."

Absalom gave her a bleak look. "For what?" he
asked. "Be glad you're healthy."

With a long sigh, she turned back to the stove
again. She's like Theodore, thought Henry; she
wants so much more than she'll get. But the age is
against her. It's against them both; but her most
of all.

He thought of the peddler who had tried to sell
him stock in the Atchison, Topeka, and Santa Fe,
and smiled. He'll get along, he thought. A lot of
them started like that, peddling . . .

He imagined how Mr. Neuberger must have appeared to Becky, dark and a little foreign, or at
least from another state, with distance and strangeness to recommend him. She's only a child, he
thought; she doesn't know what she wants.

And suddenly the sense of Eileen swept over him,
holding him breathless and still. No, he thought,
there's only one person all your life; and it's meant
to be like that.

Poor Theodore. But that couldn't be helped,
either.

CHAPTER SIX

Oɴ Sundays, the Arkbesters attended divine service at the little white church whose hollow, unhurried bell, rolling across the fields and slopes of Landons, brought back to Henry memories of his childhood. Not that he had ever thought much of God as a child, except as a sort of elderly Someone, with eyes to see in the dark, gifts for those He loved, and punishment for everybody else. The fact that neither punishment nor gift ever came his way, no matter what he did to deserve them, dulled his interest in heaven very soon; but there was something about the situation in which he now found himself which brought that early image back to him. Perhaps it was because Absalom and Ivy were on such intimate terms with divinity; which was the way he had always supposed them to have been.

Now, sitting again in the family pew between the two windows with their remembered squares of blue, yellow, and red, and listening to the preacher, the Reverend Dr. Gilpin, pleading and exhorting above him, he was more than ever reminded of that world in which men asked their own favors of God, to Whom they confided their anxieties as well as their business affairs.

Dr. Gilpin had taken as his text the 17th verse of the 6th chapter of Jeremiah: "And they shall eat up thine harvest and thy bread which thy sons and thy daughters should eat." His sermon was aimed against the city milkmen, who bought milk from the farmers at dry measure, and sold it again at liquid measure, thereby making a profit for themselves of twelve gallons in every hundred. "O God," he exclaimed, looking upward, "consider the produce of our labors. In Thy infinite goodness consider the difficulties that beset and oppress us. Teach us to know our friends; let us join with the milk producers around Philadelphia in making efforts to secure ourselves against the impositions of those who

would take advantage of us. We do not ask Thee
for profit beyond our due; but Thy Son has said, Is
not the workman worthy of his hire? Help us to see
the truth, Lord; and to do our own distributing.
Look down upon Thy children, and in Thy great
mercy bless our establishments. Bless the fruit of
our farms and the toil of our hands. Let not the
Philistine rejoice; the establishment of our hands,
bless Thou it."

Henry glanced along the pew at his family, each
with his own thoughts, and in the presence of his
God. How different the expression on each face,
and yet how alike; for they believed one thing in
common, that God's first concern was with them,
and only after that with the destiny of man. For a
moment he saw them as they were, and understood
them: John, the twelve-year-old, his mind all care-
less mischief like a ball of string, too young yet to
be afraid of the divine wrath, except at night, or in
the dark; and beside him, Becky, her ripening body
bursting with love, some of it for gentle Jesus, some
of it for the excitements of the world, but all in a
virtuous way, hungry and innocent. And then Ivy,
her face closed and stubborn; she was like a mar-

iner steering an ocean course, with heaven her
compass and her star. An unforgiving woman in a
man's world. Absalom sat beside her, a hard
farmer; God was a farmer, too, to Absalom, hard
and quiet, a strong worker, with a green hand. Next
to him sat Theodore, who wanted to travel, at least
as far as Ohio, but who wanted to marry Eileen as
well; he'd never do both, for God was no traveler,
but a strict family man, and a great one for duty.
And between them and Henry, sat the chaplain.

It was in the chaplain's face that Henry tried to
read an explanation of what he had seen. But whatever the chaplain thought, his face reflected only
a mild sympathy and a friendly concern. He neither
agreed, nor disagreed; during the sermon, indeed,
he appeared to doze. Of all here, thought Henry
with surprise, he has religion the least.

And yet he knew, without being told, that the
chaplain was a truly religious man. If I could only
see his picture of God, he thought, like I can see
Absalom's . . . then I'd know.

But though it remained a mystery, he found
comfort in the wise and gentle expression behind
which the chaplain hid his thoughts. I guess it's all

right, he told himself. People have to be the way they are. The world was different for Ivy and Absalom . . . God wasn't a farmer to me, or a compass; I don't know what He was. Maybe I'll find out some day, if I live long enough. Maybe Eileen is part of it, too.

And he murmured under his breath, "Let me have Eileen, Lord."

"There is always someone praying on the other side," remarked the chaplain in a low voice. "So someone is always disappointed."

And as Henry looked up, startled and confused, he added with a smile,

"I was thinking of the city milkmen."

The melodeon played, tremulous and brief, breathless and reedy; and in the dim and colored light, through which the age-old dust fell gently without a sound, the congregation intoned its responses. The choir stood up to sing; their voices were not very good, but they enjoyed it. " 'He leadeth me,' " they sang, soprano, tenor, and bass, " 'Oh blessed thought, Oh words with heavenly comfort fraught. Whate'er I do, where'er I be, Still 'tis God's hand that leadeth me.' "

Dr. Gilpin bowed his head above the lectern. "'May the Lord bless you and keep you,'" he said. "'May the Lord make His face to shine upon you. May the Lord lift up His gracious countenance upon you, and give you peace.'"

"Amen," said the chaplain clearly; and it seemed to Henry that his face shone with a joyous light. "A most enjoyable service," he remarked, as they rose to go. "And altogether suitable to the times."

"Well, now," said Absalom, "I don't know." He walked out ahead of his family, a sober, bearded figure in a long, dark coat, with trousers of a different material. "I got my interests more in truck, than in cows," he said.

Ivy followed him, the skirt of her best Sunday dress tight in front, and gathered into a modest bustle behind. Her cape was of soft, lined wool, her bonnet was of brown velvet. "I'd as lief he'd talked a little more about the life everlasting," she declared. "I like to be edified, on Sundays."

"The life everlasting is about as good one Sunday as another," said Absalom. "I had my mind set on a thumper, myself."

"What about, Pa?" asked John curiously.

Absalom climbed into the family surrey, and took up the reins. "I'm troubled in my mind," he said. "I could do with a good sermon on this earthly life. I'd like to hear some hope of better times ahead."

"No one can see ahead," said Ivy sensibly. "You got to put your trust in the heavenly powers."

"I know," said Absalom; "and that's all right so long as the Republicans are running the country. But suppose Greeley had been elected?"

"Well," said Ivy, "suppose he had?"

"I hate to think of it," said Absalom.

As they drove along in the quiet, noonday sunshine, the old surrey creaked and swayed over the hard ground. Ivy balanced herself gingerly in the middle seat, the new skirt, tight across her knees under the light carriage-robe, obliging her to sit very straight, and the bustle at the rear edging her forward. She was uncomfortable, it was all she could do to move, but she had a feeling of elegance proper to the occasion.

In front, Absalom continued to talk about the things that worried him. They were many, from the violence of the mill workers in the north to the low moral tone of the times, from the high taxes on farmers to the large amount of small-pox in the state. "It does seem like a visitation," he remarked. "It don't seem like things would ever come right again in the world."

But what worried him most in the end, was the stir and working in the air, the ferment of the age itself — the new roads being built, crossing the old turnpikes, opening up new country, the railways reaching out in every direction, the coming and going all about him. "I tell you," he declared, "we're making a mistake. We'd ought to stay at home and mind our own business. You take how they're looking for the North Pole; I wouldn't be surprised but one day they're going to find it. Then what will they do with it?"

"They'll use it for a marker," said Henry, "to fly over."

"Sure," said Absalom heavily; "sure. Like a bird.

"Anyway," he declared, "it's too cold up there to do any good."

Ivy adjusted the cape around her shoulders with an air of finality. "I don't know about the North Pole," she remarked, "but there's some new things, like the Young Ladies' Christian Association, that I believe in."

"That's audacious, too," said Absalom. "If you ask me, we're getting altogether too big for ourselves. If God had meant for us to spread ourselves around the world, He'd have made Englishmen out of us."

At that moment, from the roadside where he was walking, a young man in a short overcoat and embroidered vest lifted his beaver hat in a polite salute. " Now who," asked Absalom, "was that? I never saw him before."

"That was the peddler, Pa," said Theodore.

"No," said Absalom in wonder. "Well, what was he doing?"

"He's Becky's beau," said John. "Like I told you."

"Well, I'll be God dinged," said Absalom.

Sitting up straighter than ever in her seat, Ivy regarded him coldly. "Mr. Arkbester," she said.

"Yes, Ivy?" he answered, uncomfortably.

"On the Sabbath," said Ivy.

"All right," said Absalom. "But what business has he got bowing to us like he knew us?"

"He seemed purely polite to me," said Ivy.

And she added firmly,

"Such a lot of fuss about nothing."

Henry looked back at Becky. On the girl's face was an expression of surprise, of joy, and of fright; and Henry, remembering the dark, handsome eyes of Mr. Neuberger, pursed his lips in a soundless whistle.

CHAPTER SEVEN

I N the early evening, when the woods and fields were already blue with dusk, Henry sat on the kitchen steps, cleaning an old-fashioned fowling piece. With him was the chaplain; the kitchen lamp, behind them, made a yellow oblong of light in the doorway, and in front of them they saw the cold green of the western sky, with the new moon like a silver horn, and the evening star.

"I suppose I ought to worry more," said Henry, sighting back along the barrel at the light which glinted on the oiled and shiny steel, "but all the time I have this feeling that it's all right. It's as if somebody was trying to tell me something; only I didn't ask any questions."

He looked at the chaplain doubtfully. "I don't know the answer yet," he said.

The chaplain did not reply at once. "No," he said at last, "you could hardly expect to."

He continued thoughtfully: "A man's own life is all-important to him. He tastes, touches, sees, hears . . . and thinks of himself as the center of the universe. That is only natural, because he cannot taste, or hear, or see for anybody else. His pain is his own, he cannot even describe it. And in the dark, closed-in cells of his brain, his thoughts are as much alone as bodies buried in the ground.

"But all around him, in space and in time, are others like him; and when he speaks, they can hear him. So perhaps he is not the center of anything, after all."

"Then what is he?" asked Henry.

"No one knows," replied the chaplain. "The answer hasn't been given yet." And he added, smiling, "Do you understand, Corporal?"

"No, sir," said Henry simply.

"I thought not," said the chaplain.

Henry cocked the gun, and let the hammer fall

back into place with a click. "My folks worry a lot," he said. "Like what will we do with the North Pole when we find it. Still, I can see how it looked to them. But you can't explain it."

"That's what I mean," said the chaplain.

"It makes me want to laugh," said Henry, "but it's sort of sad, too. Like Absalom, wanting to see hope ahead. But he doesn't want to look ahead, to see it."

"He is human," said the chaplain.

"He'd rather look backwards," said Henry.

"Wherever he looks," said the chaplain, "he will find change and hope, doubt and perplexity. So perhaps it doesn't matter.

"Do you understand now?"

"No, sir," said Henry.

He rose to his feet, the gun under his arm. "I'm going to hang this gun back on the nail," he said. "I'll be out again."

With the fowling piece hanging once more on the wall in his great-grandfather's office, Henry came out again into the misty blue, November evening. The chaplain was gone, but in his place, hesitant and uncertain, one slippered foot on the kitchen steps, stood Eileen, a dark cape around her shoulders, and a soft woolen fascinator over her hair. "I came with Theo," she said. "He's gone to put the horse in the barn."

And she added shyly, with satisfaction,

"I was asked for supper."

He thought that he had never seen anything more lovely than her young face, shadowy in the dusk, under the woolen scarf. "Aren't you coming in?" he asked.

She shook her head. "No," she said, with a little laugh that was more like a catch of breath, "not yet. I'm afraid to go in without Theo. Mrs. Arkbester — she scares me. Isn't that awful? Come and sit down with me here, while I wait."

They sat together on the steps; their shoulders touched, he breathed the faint fragrance of young skin and hair, of homemade soap, and lavender. "I looked for you in church," he said. "But I didn't see you."

"I was there," she told him; "and I saw you. Our pew is five rows back. I thought you'd turn around, but you didn't. Uncle Cyrus likes to come late, and go early. You didn't look around once."

"I guess I didn't," he said. "I guess I was afraid to."

She laughed again, a light peal in the twilight. "I didn't think a soldier would be afraid of anything," she said.

"It's been so long since I went to church," said Henry, "I was afraid of how to act."

"Oh," she said; and her voice was shocked and unbelieving. "I'm sorry," she said.

"Why?" asked Henry in surprise.

"You ought to go to church more regularly," she said solemnly. "You oughtn't ever to miss a single Sunday."

Once again, as at their first meeting, Henry felt himself flooded with a sensation of innocence and joy. He remembered the morning happiness of those days when, as a child, life had seemed fresh, mysterious, and beautiful; and he exclaimed earnestly,

"I'll try to go to church more often."

At the same time he understood that this religious conversation was wholly for the sake of the young woman to whom he wished to bind himself as closely as possible by the bonds of the spirit.

He wished to feel as she did, to see the world through her eyes; he longed to get up at the same hour each morning, and go with her to church on Sundays. The thought that he might be included in her prayers caused him a pang of exquisite joy, tempered by the fear that he might be unworthy.

"Well, tell me," she said; "do you like being a soldier?"

The question, so unexpected, caught him by surprise. "There wasn't much choice," he said, without thinking. "They just took me."

"Oh," she said; and looked away. He felt that she was disappointed in him, that she had expected a different kind of answer. And all at once he wanted to justify himself, and to explain everything. "They took us all," he said. "Everybody had to go."

She nodded. "I know," she said. "It was the draft. I read about it; and about the riots they had."

"There weren't any riots," he said stupidly. "I don't know what you're talking about."

"I read about them," she said; "but it doesn't matter. Tell me what you're going to do when you get out of the army."

And she added with a light laugh, "I suppose there's a lady friend somewhere."

"There was," he said. "But now there's another."

Her face was hidden from him; in the dusk, he couldn't tell what she was thinking. He took her hand, and she let it lie for a moment in his, before she drew it away. It was small and soft; and when he put his own hand to his face a moment later, his fingers smelled faintly of dried rose leaves. "I know about you, anyway," he said.

She did not answer at once. "You mean about Theo?" she said at last; and when he nodded, she added,

"I guess everybody expects it."

"Do you expect it, too?" he asked. He had trouble making his voice sound airy, the way he wanted it to; he felt cold and nervous.

"I don't know," she answered. "I like Theo." She glanced at him quickly, out of the corner of her eye. "He's very nice," she said. "He does everything I want."

"What do you want, Eileen?" asked Henry.

She leaned closer to him, and her voice grew slow and sweet, and full of relish, like molasses.

"I want," she said, "Oh — I want a lot of things. I want a house, with a porch like Uncle Cyrus', only nicer. And I want a hired girl, and a sewing machine . . . all my own. And a canary bird. And a marble wash-stand."

"What else do you want?" he asked.

"Oh," she said, "I don't know." She looked around at him candidly in the evening light. " Just the nice things," she said.

"What about you, Henry?"

He wanted to answer, You; but he didn't say it. He couldn't, he thought — not with Theodore coming back any minute from the barn, and supper still ahead, with the whole family watching. He wasn't afraid of Theodore, but he was a little afraid of Ivy.

He said, with wonder, "I feel like I'd known you ever since I can remember. Like we'd been kids together."

"Yes," she said slowly, "it's funny; you look familiar to me, too. More even than Theo — though you're cousins. Why is that, Henry? Sometimes when you say things, it's almost like I knew what you were going to say."

"I guess it's fate," he declared. He heard her sigh

happily; he could feel the soft curve of her shoulder against his arm, as she moved closer to him on the steps.

"We could almost be brother and sister," she said. "Couldn't we?"

"That isn't what I meant," he said. And yet he knew that she was right. For where was there any strangeness in his feeling about her?

"Do you know *On A May-day Morning*?" she asked. "It's my favorite song."

And in a low voice, sweet, breathless, and a little out of tune, she sang,

> " '*I try to forget him, but all in vain,*
> *On a May-day morning early,*
> *And if I never should see him again,*
> *It will break my heart, or nearly.*' "

"It's pretty," he said.

The evening deepened around them, the green sky faded and darkened, the stars appeared one by one. A fox barked far off on the mountain, and a dog answered from across the valley. The hush of the night, the fading sky and the bright, sinking moon, the cold air with its faint smell of earth, of wood-smoke and dung, made a mystery and a silence around him, and his heart filled with long-ing for the world's beauty, for the immemorial hush of evening, for young girls singing in the dusk, and for the cold, sweet air of nightfall in other lands, in other years, far off and forgotten . . . over the same brown earth, under the same white moon.

He trembled; he thought that she, too, trembled against him. "Do you like me?" he asked shakily.

She only nodded, not looking at him; he saw the curve of her cheek, the slender line of her chin; he felt like weeping with happiness, his throat ached, and he exclaimed,

"I like you, too, Eileen."

For a moment their fingers clung together like dandelion seed. Then, without speaking, they rose and entered the house, as Theodore came whistling from the barn.

For the rest of the evening, Henry was scarcely aware of what he did or said, or of the others around him. He saw his family only vaguely: Absalom, un-comfortable in a high wing collar complete with string tie, his long trousers tucked off the floor inside his boots, his bearded chin bent hungrily over his plate; the children, John and Becky, silent, with wide eyes, staring at the guest, missing nothing; Ivy, quiet and watchful, but friendly, doing her best for Theodore who was all awkward blushes and eager agreement. But not for a moment did Henry lose sight of Eileen — Eileen with her hair like a dark, shiny cloud in the lamplight, and her cheeks shadowed and rosy by turns as she smiled first at one and then at another. She filled the room with her presence; and from her clear voice and dainty gestures there exhaled an indefinable fragrance of youth and delight. Once, and only once, her eyes met his across the table . . . across a chasm deeper than the sea, wider than time, darker than the night; and as her eyes widened and held, his heart strained outward in his breast like a captive balloon.

It was almost as if fire had flamed there for a moment in the air between them. Dazed and a little frightened, he looked around him, but no one else seemed to have been aware of it. No one, that is, but the chaplain; when Henry looked at him, he was smiling — a little sadly, Henry thought.

CHAPTER EIGHT

I̲ᴛ was a quiet morning the fresh, mountain air warm in the sun and icy in the shadows, sweet with the smell of grapes over-ripe on the vines, and the winey smell of apples from the press behind the barn, where Absalom was pressing out the last cider of the season. Autumn brightness lay everywhere, over the brown earth and the dark pines, the bare trees and the silvery fields, over the barn from which came the sounds of a horse patiently stamping, and over the old, brick smoke-house from which a plume of faint, blue, hickory smoke ascended like an Indian pipe in the still air.

Absalom himself was at the cider press, his foot on the treadle, while Theodore brought from the great pile of half-rotten apples, bushel after bushel of russet-colored greenings, and speckled Mackintoshes. Ivy was in the kitchen, making soap; and Henry sat peacefully by the kitchen window, watching and listening and dreaming; and thinking — when he thought at all — the old thoughts of his childhood, of peace and of plenty.

As thoughts, they were neither happy, nor unhappy. Eileen was in them, woven through them like a bright ribbon, here, there, and everywhere. She was the little girl who used to live over the hill, whose desk was across the room at school, whom he had never dared speak to. She was the young girl whose voice he used to hear whispering on porches in the evening, behind the lilacs and the honeysuckle. A child, a girl whom he had never met, whom he had always known . . .

He watched a red squirrel come out from underneath the woodshed, and flirt away across the yard; he saw a flicker swoop down from a tree, and search the ground for food. It's late for a flicker, he thought, but there hasn't been a frost yet, not a black frost. He remembered how he used to see the red-winged blackbirds when he was a boy, and how once he had heard a brown bird singing like a canary, and somebody had told him that it was a mocking bird. That song had a sharper tune to it, he thought, for being so far away from home.

On the stove, the big, three-gallon iron cauldron of rain water simmered and bubbled. The pound of saponifier was already dissolved in it, and Ivy was measuring out the four pounds of tallow. In the rain-water barrel by the door, twelve more gallons of good, soft rain water stood waiting to be added to the mixture, once it was clear. "That's the way my mother made her soap," Ivy remarked, "and it does pretty good."

She went back to the kitchen rocker, and began to rock herself slowly up and down. For all the bright weather, her health was a little poorly that morning, and she thought a bad spell of rain was on the way. "I can tell from my rheumatics," she declared. "They twinge me in advance."

She peered at Henry with her head to one side, the way she had. "Bright skies can't fool me," she said; and heaved a light sigh. "You wouldn't care to give me a hand with this soap, Henry?" she said.

He roused himself from his day-dreaming with an effort. "You want me to put the tallow in for you, Cousin Ivy?" he asked.

She got up, and limped across the room to peer into the boiling pot. "Yes," she said; "you put it in, nice and slow; and stir it round." She went back to her chair again, and wiped the little moisture of steam off her face with a cotton handkerchief. "I like a lot of soap," she declared. "I like to see things clean; it comforts me."

The coal and hickory fire threw a warm, golden glow half-way across the room; the odor of tallow was strong and thick. Bending over the stove, Henry heard Ivy sigh again. "My children don't like things clean the way I do," she said, "though I declare I've tried to bring them up the same as me. That Becky — sometimes you wouldn't hardly guess she was a well-brought-up girl at all. She figures no one's ever going to see behind her ears; but I say and I say to her, who is going to know who's liable to come walking in at any minute? Life is full of surprises; when I met Absalom, it was a surprise to us both. I was out in the yard, hanging up a pair of my mother's petticoats to dry. I remember I

didn't take to him much at first, but he looked better
the second time. He'd got himself slicked up a little.
I wore a hoop in those days."

She rocked up and down, quietly and happily.
"Yes," she said, almost as though she were talking
to herself, comforting herself with the good things
she remembered, "Absalom and me, we brought
this farm up from next to nothing. We brought it
up from pretty near wild land; we plowed and
we hewed, and we made a living. Sometimes we'd
do a little better, or sometimes a little worse, but
it all evened up in the end. My mother, she gave me
her recipes. She knew them all by heart, anyway."

She put her hand up to feel for a stray wisp of
hair. "That Becky," she said; "she won't be happy
till she has a cake of sweet-smelling store soap for
her hands. I tell her who cares how her hands smell,
so long as they're clean? I tell her, you want to smell
a little extra good, you got your sachet powder. So
then she says her sachet powder isn't strong enough
to smell up a mouse.

"Take a look is that liquor clear yet, or not."

Henry peered dubiously into the cauldron. "No
ma'am," he said; "there's lumps in it."

"That's the eyes," said Ivy comfortably. "Well, we've got plenty of time. There's no hurry."

For a while there was no sound, except the bubbling of the pot on the stove, and the small, steady squeak of the rocking chair as Ivy rocked herself up and down. "It's funny the way you think of things," she said presently. "You take this farm we worked so hard over. It'll go to the children when we're gone, and my mother's recipes along with it. I wouldn't have it otherwise; to think that strangers might get it, would purely faze me. I like to think of things passing down from hand to hand, from mother to son and son to daughter; it keeps me from being afraid at night. Though I hope to see my Maker face to face in the hereafter, and also our Blessed Savior. Still, come night, I get the horrors sometimes."

Henry leaned over the warm stove, slowly stirring the soap. He heard her, and he didn't hear her, all at the same time; he stood dreaming, his thoughts going on from where they had left off, among the evening honeysuckle. He remembered the boy in school, the dusty classroom, the smell of chalk and ink; he remembered the autumn games, the sound of the booted ball, the songs and the cheers; they were like sounds from far away, cheerful and small. He remembered spring, and the yellow leaves of the forsythia, the smell of lilacs in the rain, of tar and oil on the roads. He remembered the jalopies at the post office, and his friends meeting and greeting each other in the yellow lamplight. He remembered the drug store where they used to sit together over their cokes, the laughter and the cries. And a girl he had known — was her name Eileen? — who had promised to wait for him . . .

The far-off voices of his youth; the sweet, the shy, the bright, young voices. America . . .

He thought of a poem he had read in school, by a great poet who had died young, and who had loved his land and his people. He could only remember a little of it.

" If there can be a heaven, let it wear
Even such an air.
Not shamed with sun nor black without a ray,
But gently day."

CHAPTER NINE

John had been kept home from school to help bale hay. With Theodore and Absalom, he wove the bales with heavy flax, and carried them in the wagon to the barn. Absalom hadn't much livestock, but he could always use his hay, or sell it.

So Henry drove to the store that day, to get the mail, a spool of black darning cotton, and a book of cut-out patterns for Ivy; and a pot of Dr. Clark's Sweet-Scented Hair Pomade for Theodore. He found Mr. Simon, the storekeeper and postmaster, behind the counter, weighing out dozens of hoarhound drops from a glass jar. "Well, sir," said Mr. Simon cheerfully, "we're having a nice spell of weather."

The hard, brown candies made a sound like shot

against the tin tray of the weighing machine. "Yes, sir," said Mr. Simon, "it's cool and dry. After a hot summer, and windy, too; the hottest and windiest I can remember. Getting ready for winter colds and quinsies; I like to be prepared. What can I do for you?"

Henry told him. When he mentioned the pomade for Theodore, Mr. Simon chuckled. "The young fellows nowadays," he declared; "there's no beating them. They're cards, that's what they are; beauing around to beat hell. I guess Theodore's got his eyes set on the young lady across the valley. Don't blame him, either; now that's a sweet young girl if ever I saw one."

"Yes," said Henry shortly. "And a spool of darning cotton."

"I see where Horace Greeley is sick," said Mr. Simon, rummaging behind the counter, "and like to die. Plumb irritated to death, I guess."

Henry made no answer to this remark, which meant nothing to him in any case. Coming up with the darning cotton in his hand, Mr. Simon declared solemnly,

"It is the end of the Democratic Party."

He gave Henry a wink. "They thought we had a low moral tone," he said.

Henry gazed into the glass case on the counter. Licorice, he said to himself, and rock candy. And peppermint sticks. The names came into his mind, without his having to think about them.

"I see," said Mr. Simon hopefully, "where they're going to award us damages of three-four million, in the Alabama case. The question is — will we get it? I never knew England to give us anything yet."

He shook his head. "You take France," he said. "There she is; and what's going to happen to her? It all depends on one old man."

"Not any more," said Henry.

"No?" said Mr. Simon in surprise. He looked at Henry curiously. "You're not from around here, mister, are you?" he asked.

"I used to be," said Henry. "There's been some changes."

Mr. Simon nodded his head. "I knew you were a relative of the family," he declared, "but I couldn't figure where from. Now I recollect there was an Arkbester moved out in '63. He had a mortgage took up on him."

He heaved a deep and comfortable sigh. "Yes, sir," he announced, "there's been big changes hereabouts. You never saw the Grange Hall before; I'll lay a bet to that. Or the brick front to the Bank."

"I never did," said Henry.

Using his chin to hold the paper down, Mr. Simon tied up Henry's purchases with a piece of string. "Here's your bundle, mister," he said. "You tell Ivy I've got some arrowroot and quince water, does she want it; and you tell her I'll have a bottle of Wolcott's Pain Paint for her next week."

"What's the matter with her," asked Henry; "is she sick?"

Mr. Simon looked at him with a sort of pity. "No more than any female," he declared. "But they all like to dose themselves. It gives them courage to continue."

Henry took his bundle, and drove off. It was time for school to be out, and he planned to pick up Becky on the way home. He felt a friendly curiosity toward this young girl, with whom he had hardly exchanged more than a few words; and he looked forward to meeting her along the road.

He saw her ahead of him as he rounded the

curve at Landons Corners. She was walking slowly, by the road's edge; but she was not alone. Close beside her, his dark head bent in earnest conversation, and with a tender air, walked Mr. Neuberger.

Hearing the sound of wheels behind her, Becky looked.fearfully around, shrank to one side, uttered a faint scream, and hid her face behind her school books. But when she saw that Henry was alone, she took courage, and peeked out again, over the top. "You want a ride home?" he asked.

The peddler, whose face had grown a little paler, drew himself up, and lifted his hat in a polite gesture. "I trust," he said, "that you will not think too badly of this meeting, Mr. Arkbester. It was only an accident; no impoliteness was intended."

"It's no business of mine," said Henry shortly.

The peddler blinked at him for a moment in silence. "So," he said finally, "so . . . but just the same, I assure you . . ."

"It's nothing to me," said Henry, "one way or another." And motioning to the seat beside him, he added,

"Hop in, Becky."

She climbed — a little unwillingly, he noticed —

up over the wheel, and sat down as far away from him as she could. Mr. Neuberger stood below them in the road, his hat in his hand, and his eyes fixed upon the girl in a look at once ardent and solicitous. She stared down at him solemnly. "Good-by," she said; "Mr. Neuberger."

"Good-by," he said bravely. Then, collecting himself, he turned to Henry with a dignified air. "I have nothing but respect for the young lady," he declared.

"Naturally," said Henry. And he added carelessly,

"How's the Santa Fe getting along?"

At once Mr. Neuberger's face changed, his expression lightened, and he assumed a brisk manner. "There is a great future in the West," he said earnestly. "It is impossible to be wrong about it." Reaching into one of the inner pockets of his voluminous coat, he drew out some papers, and looked at them with surprise. "No," he said with vexation, "this is not it. However," he added hopefully, "could I interest you in the prospectus for a new writing machine?"

Smiling, Henry waved him aside, and shook the

reins over the horse's back. "I'll be seeing you," he said.

Mr. Neuberger stood by the roadside, looking after the retreating wagon. "A book of home remedies?" he called after them, in a half-hearted voice; but they were already too far away to hear him. With a sigh, he put his papers back in his pocket again, and turned away. " 'Das ewig Weibliche,' " he whispered, " 'zieht uns hinan.' "

The wagon rolled up the road in silence, except for its own creaks and noises. After a while, Becky slid over closer to Henry, and put her lunch box down between her feet. "Cousin Henry," she began; and then stopped. She seemed unhappy, and uncertain.

"Yes," he said, encouraging her.

"Were you really in California?" she asked at last.

"I've been almost everywhere," said Henry.

"In India?" she asked breathlessly.

"Well, no," he said. "But I've been in Australia."

"Oh my," she whispered. "Australia."

"We had an army there," said Henry.

"Did we?" she said. "I didn't know. Cousin Henry . . ."

"Yes?"

"Have you ever been to Philadelphia?"

"No," said Henry.

She took a deep breath. "I wish I could go to Philadelphia," she said. "I wish I could live in a big city, and wear nice clothes, and be refined.

"Like Eileen," she added.

"I don't think Eileen was ever in Philadelphia," said Henry.

"Well," said Becky, "she's been in Wheeling, West Virginia, anyway."

She was silent for a moment, her hands clasped in her lap, her eyes dreaming out over the fields. The wagon rolled slowly up the road, the wheels creaked, the horse's hoofs sounded clear and loud in the still air. "Cousin Henry," she said.

"Now what?" he asked.

"Were you ever in love?"

"Who, me?" said Henry. "You hadn't ought to ask questions like that."

"No, but really," she insisted. "Were you, ever?"

"Yes," said Henry.

"Tell me," she said, "what's it feel like? Because . . . nobody will tell me."

"Oh, I don't know," said Henry vaguely. "I guess it doesn't feel very good."

She nodded wisely. "That's it," she declared.

"You're too young to be in love," said Henry kindly. "You've got growing pains, is all."

"No," she said; "I know growing pains. I had them last year. Only," she went on, with a tremor in her voice, "how can you dass to be in love with somebody your ma and pa don't know about? I mean . . . if they wouldn't like him?"

Henry shook his head. "Are you sure you haven't got things mixed up?" he asked; "like wanting to live in a strange place, and to marry the first strange man you see?"

"No," said Becky; "it isn't just because he's strange. He's very educated; and he's traveled all over. Not," she added hurriedly, "as far as you, maybe . . . But tell me Cousin Henry — do girls in Australia feel the same way I do?"

"I don't know," said Henry. "I don't know the way you feel."

"I feel all achey," said Becky simply.

"Well," said Henry, "I'm sorry for you."

"It's him I'm sorry for," said Becky. "He's had a sad life."

"He'll have a sadder one if your pa catches him," said Henry.

"I know," she said. "That makes me feel worse."

"Look," said Henry earnestly; "you want to be careful. A girl like you can get herself into a heap of trouble. Why don't you have a talk with your ma?"

She turned her young, serious eyes on him. "Ma wouldn't like that," she said. "It wouldn't be re-fined."

There was no bitterness in the remark, only lone-liness and uncertainty. "It was different when Ma was a girl," she said. "I don't know why, but it was. Ma didn't want to go anywhere, or do anything . . . like I do. I guess she was always happy with her lot."

It was hard to think of Ivy as a young girl — though for that matter it had been hard once upon a time to picture her at all. And not so long ago she had been Becky's age, and maybe with an eye for Absalom . . . though what she could have seen in him, Henry couldn't for the life of him imagine. Was it a home — a house and a family? Perhaps it had been the farm itself, the good earth . . . Security, Henry thought; it used to mean a lot, once. So many things used to mean a lot; but after a while some of them didn't mean so much any more. Only a few things were worth holding on to; only a few of the many hopes and fears were ever passed from one generation to another. "Life, liberty, and the pursuit of happiness . . ." "With malice toward none; with charity for all . . ."

Peace and bread, work and children. The old, American dream . . .

"Ivy knows her own mind," said Henry. "I'll say that much for her."

"She thinks the President is awful, because he smokes seegars," said Becky thoughtfully. "But Pa chews tobacco, and she doesn't dass say a word."

She folded her young hands virtuously across her lap. "Mr. Neuberger doesn't smoke or chew," she announced. "He's going to be a merchant some day."

Homeward bound, the horse trotted briskly forward; and Henry let the reins hang loose in his fingers. A curious feeling, half sadness, half solace, took possession of him. How lonely each life appeared, set apart from its fellows in time and space; how unreal the lives of others, how vain their anxieties, how small their differences. And yet . . . what infinite communion.

And in a prophetic mood, he exclaimed,
"Don't do it, Becky."

She did not answer; but it seemed to him that her eyes widened for a moment with a look of fear.

CHAPTER TEN

I T was only natural that the Rev. Dr. Gilpin should pay a call at the Arkbesters, to visit with Ivy, and to meet the chaplain. Seated together in the parlor with its shiny, horsehair sofa, its stiff, embroidered chairs, its cabinet of bric-a-brac and shells, and the table with its heavy, woven cloth, they gazed at each other politely, and munched on ginger cookies from a jar.

"I believe that I saw you at Sunday service," said Dr. Gilpin. "I would have called upon you earlier, but the press of my duties did not permit me the pleasure. It might interest you to know that I, too, served for a time as chaplain with our armed forces; with the Fourth Pennsylvania, to be exact. I must say that our uniform differed somewhat from yours.

However, after Bull Run, I returned home, to comfort my congregation."

"I don't know as we could have gone on without him," said Ivy, "through the dark times."

"Today," said Dr. Gilpin, "I am the shepherd of a troubled flock, whose members look to me for guidance in an uncertain world."

And he smiled at the chaplain as though to say, You understand my problems.

But the chaplain looked thoughtful. "For an uncertain world," he said, "it seems to me to have a great many firm convictions."

"Convictions," replied Dr. Gilpin; "yes. But righteousness? No."

"I do not always know what righteousness is," said the chaplain.

Both Ivy and the Rev. Dr. Gilpin stared at him in surprise; then the minister cleared his throat. "Well," he said; "hm."

"I must say," remarked Ivy.

The chaplain made an outward gesture with his hands. "I was thinking of what a man owes his neighbors," he said mildly.

"Yes," said Dr. Gilpin; "yes." He grew thoughtful, and gazed at the wall with a solemn expression. "A man should exercise a certain care," he said after a while, "in picking his neighbors."

"Surely," said the chaplain, "we are all neighbors to one another?"

"Only in a sense," said Dr. Gilpin with conviction; "only in a sense. I do not consider the criminal, or the depraved, in such a light. Nor do I expect to find them my neighbors in the hereafter."

He continued:

"Shall we forgive the Democrats for their slanderous attack upon the Administration?"

"It will soon be forgotten," said the chaplain.

"Never," said Dr. Gilpin stoutly. "'Suppose ye that I am come to give peace on earth? I tell you Nay; but rather division.'"

"'A house divided against a house falleth,'" said the chaplain; "which is also from Luke."

"True," said Dr. Gilpin. "But they ought not to take advantage of us. Allow me."

And reaching across the chaplain, he extracted another ginger cookie from the jar.

"I am speaking of certain milk dealers in the

cities of Philadelphia and Harrisburg," he explained. And he added, in ringing tones,

"Let us not lose the fruits of our victory."

"Victory," said the chaplain thoughtfully; "that is a beautiful and a terrible word. For it carries with it great responsibilities, not only to the future, but to the past. It is not enough to plan for peace; the victor must try to remember the nature of his enemy."

"It is the nature of the rich," declared Dr. Gilpin, "to become more so."

"Then do not quarrel with them for that reason," said the chaplain, "but for other reasons. Let us quarrel with the evil in man's nature, not with the whole nature of man. Thus, little by little, we shall effect an improvement."

"Sometimes," said Dr. Gilpin, "when I read about such things as the Ku Klux Klan, or the Pattenburg Massacre, I wonder if it is possible to improve mankind at all. Perhaps it would have been better to have left things as they were. . . . It is likely that freeing the slaves was the beginning, rather than the end, of our problems."

"Freedom is always a beginning," said the chaplain. "It is true that very solid problems sometimes arise from great spiritual movements. Yet the spirit will not be denied. Neither by the skeptics, nor by the conquerors."

"I should like to believe you," said Dr. Gilpin. "But I have found that God helps him who helps himself."

"That is true," agreed the chaplain, "although, like most sayings, a great deal depends on what you make of it. There are remedies for all the ills of man, but we must find them for ourselves."

"Some remedies make me feel real good," said Ivy; and went on to describe a cure for cancer, scrofula, and rheumatism, by the name of Cundurango, for which she had sent all the way to New York City. "We all have our cross to bear," she remarked.

"Amen," said Dr. Gilpin.

"What we have to bear," said the chaplain, "is in proportion to what we love. He who loves little, suffers only for himself; while he who loves men greatly, bears their sufferings in his heart."

"Ah," said Dr. Gilpin. He placed the tips of his fingers together, and studied them for a moment in silence. "A very true remark," he said at last. " 'Build thee more stately mansions, O my soul.' "

"Still," he went on, thoughtfully, "one cannot love everybody, everywhere. 'Thou shalt be as a light unto the Gentiles.' "

The chaplain smiled. "Do you love your country, Dr. Gilpin?" he asked.

"Naturally," said Dr. Gilpin.

"Yet America is a wide country," said the chaplain, "and the heart must be wide to love it truly. There must be room in it for forest and plain, for the cypress swamp, and the snow. Do you love the mountains, Dr. Gilpin, the level prairies, the buckwheat and the corn? Do you love the windy hills of San Francisco, the iron balconies of New Orleans, the slender, white houses of Charleston facing the sea?"

"I have not had your advantages of travel, sir," said Dr. Gilpin stiffly.

"I love what I know," said Ivy. "I love Lebanon County, Pennsylvania."

"To love America," continued the chaplain gently, "is to love American voices and American faces, the dark and the light, the brisk and the slow. It is to love American jokes and laughter, American song, the levee chanteys and the Methodist hymns. It is to love the wine and apple air of autumn, the smoke of eucalyptus fires, the smell of sage at evening, the sound of the mocking bird. It is to remember the Indian and the buffalo, the herds of Texas cattle, and the first Thanksgiving. It is to see God in the sky; but to see the Kingdom of Heaven here on earth."

Dr. Gilpin cleared his throat. "At least," he said drily, "you do not ask us to love the Mormons, or the Jews."

"You will need to do that, also," said the chaplain.

In the shocked silence which followed, Henry rose to his feet. He could hear Ivy draw in her breath; he almost thought he could hear Dr. Gilpin's knuckles crack as he pressed them together. "If you folks'll excuse me," he said, "I'm going out and shoot me some rabbits."

With Absalom's old fowling piece once more under his arm, he let himself out of the kitchen door, and started across the yard, where a few hens were pecking aimlessly at the bare ground. Down by the barn, he found the boy, John, whittling at a wagon trace which had worn loose. "Hello," he said. "You want to go along after rabbits?"

"Can't do it," said John. "Pa would whup the tar out of me, didn't I fix this trace for him."

He looked up inquisitively. "What they talking about in there?" he asked. "Me?"

"You?" asked Henry. "No. Why would they be?"

"Well," said John, "they're always fixing to save me."

"From what?" asked Henry.

"From hell, I guess," said the boy solemnly. "But I don't know. Anyway, I ain't scared of hell . . . much."

"What are you scared of then?" asked Henry.

"Pa," said John. "And night-riders. And thunder-storms."

He wove a wire through the trace, and bound it round with hemp. "Cousin Henry," he said hopefully.

"Yes?"

"Did you ever see a Magic Lantern?"

Henry thought for a moment; a magic lantern. Well, as a matter of fact, he never did. "No," he said.

John took a deep breath. "I'm going to get me one

someday," he announced. "When I save up as much as five dollars." He gazed at Henry with simple joy. "You see all kinds of colored pictures in it," he said.

"Five dollars is a lot of money," said Henry.

"Yes," John agreed, "it is. You know how I'm going to get that five dollars? I'm going to be an agent, that's how I'm going to get it. I'm going to be an agent for this book, *The Destruction of Chicago*. I wrote them, and said I'd be one.

"I bet that was an awful destruction," he added happily.

Henry looked around him at the peaceful fields shining in the sun, the bright slopes and the dark trees clear and sharp against the sky. "There's been a lot of destruction," he said, "and nobody knows the end of it. Warsaw and Singapore, Coventry and Stalingrad; Chicago, too?"

"I don't know about those other places," said John slowly, "but Boston burned. Not so much as Chicago, but it burned, all right.

"You think they'll ever get built up again?"

"I guess so," said Henry. "Yes, I guess they will."

The boy nodded his head soberly; his eyes were full of dreams. "I guess I'll never get a chance to see any ruins, or anything," he said. He seemed disappointed, on the whole.

"You know what I wish? I wisht I was an Indian fighter."

Henry looked down at him; he looked at him for a long time. And in his mind he saw the relentless push of the young nation to the westward, he saw the railroads reaching out across the land, he saw the brown tide of the buffalo ebbing away across the prairies, he saw the Sioux and the Blackfeet, the Crow, the Apache, he saw Custer and the plains of the Little Big Horn. "One of my friends," he said at last, "was a Blackfoot. He died at Faid Pass.

"He died for us; for you and me. And for America. It's funny, isn't it."

He turned the old gun over in his hands, and the sunlight gleamed for a moment white and clear along the barrel. "Yes," he said, "they build the ruins up again. They build the cities over, greater and more beautiful. . . . And what the people love and want, they build that over, too.

"We only see a little of it."

CHAPTER ELEVEN

THE WOODS were very quiet as Henry went through them. But under the quiet, he could hear the woods-sounds, the little chime of water dropping, the snap of a twig, the far-off caw of crows, and the sound of silence itself, like a breath held in. The sun seemed to make a misty brightness in the air; and he thought to himself, with wonder, This is death walking with a gun in the woods. A chipmunk flirted up a tree, and scolded from a branch; he heard a dog bark far away, but he saw no rabbits. He was surprised, but he was not disappointed.

Near Bitter's Ravine, he let himself down onto what was left of an old stone wall, and sat for a while in the sun, the gun between his knees. The spot was familiar to him, although he did not know why; he thought that he had been there before, long ago, or perhaps he had been there lately. He gave up puzzling about it after a while; there was so much he kept forgetting.

He remembered a few things. He remembered what it was like to fly; he remembered the green, hot, Pacific islands, the ocean breaking on the reefs, the sound of machine guns . . . he remembered the American summers of his childhood, the sound of bells across the valley, the brown waters of Craik's Creek flowing past his knees. But what he had felt, then — what he had loved, and wanted, he forgot.

Though there had been Eileen . . .

There had always been Eileen. The name itself was part of his childhood, it went back to the beginnings. It was a boy's music . . . Eileen; it was like children talking together in the evening, a duet within his blood. It made him feel as if he were a part of some long-spaced tenderness, some endless, familiar love.

It was no surprise to see her coming toward him through the woods. She wore a green dolman and a brown, hooded bonnet, from under which her dark curls, no longer pinned high, fell to her shoulders. She walked with easy grace in her skirt of brown wool; too loose to be fashionable, it touched the ground as she moved, and gathered tiny twigs and bits of leaf along its hem.

He sat and watched her with a sense of quiet comfort. That they should be there together in the sun and the silence, seemed inevitable. She did not see him until she was almost on top of him; then she stopped, and her hands flew to her throat. "Oh," she breathed; "you frightened me."

"I didn't aim to," he said.

She came slowly closer, smiling and watching him. "You've got a gun," she said reproachfully. "You've been hunting." She didn't actually say, Oh the poor rabbits, but she might as well have.

He looked up at her curiously. Had he really been hunting? he wondered. He would have said that he had been waiting, and remembering. He lifted the gun onto his lap, and ran his hand over the satiny wood of the stock. "It's a funny old gun," he said. "But I guess it would do the business, at that."

"Men are always hunting and killing," she said.

She came up to the wall beside him, and felt the warm stone with her hand. "I'm going to sit down with you for a little," she said, "if you don't mind."

"Yes," he said. It was hard to think of anything more to say, because words only got in the way between them. It wasn't what they said that ever seemed to matter, it was the way they felt. "I knew you'd come," he said.

"Did you? But how could you have?"

"Maybe I just hoped it," he said.

She raised her arms, to toss the curls back from her shoulders. "It's funny, Henry," she said; "I hardly know anything about you at all. Who you are, or anything. Uncle Cyrus asked me yesterday, and I couldn't even tell him. He said he hadn't ever heard of your branch of the family."

She looked at him earnestly, with troubled, brown eyes. "You never did tell me about yourself really," she said.

"Does it make any difference?" he asked.

"I don't know." Frowning a little, she looked away, and a faint color came into her cheeks. "It might," she said.

"Well," he declared, "I don't know what I can

tell you. You wouldn't ever have heard of my mother or father. Or me, either. No one around here would have. Still and all, we come from here. Right here, at Landons Corners."

He pointed with his thumb, over his shoulder. "You take the farm," he said. "We're going to own it, some day."

She gave a deep sigh of satisfaction. "Well," she said; "that's different, I guess."

"Why is it different?" he asked jealously.

"Oh, I don't know," she said. She swung her feet up and down, and hummed a little tune under her breath. "It just is," she said.

He stood the gun, barrel up, against the wall. "I don't know about you, either," he remarked, "when you come right down to it."

"Me?" she cried lightly. "La! I'm just a female."

Her mood had changed like sudden weather. Now she was all sun and wheedle, and set to tease him. "Females are so uninteresting," she said. "Don't you think so, Mr. Arkbester? I know that's what you men think about us. Or are you afraid to say?

"But lady friends are different, aren't they? It's

too bad you haven't one any more. Or maybe you have; I declare, I've purely forgotten."

"Look," said Henry unhappily; "I never said . . ."

"Though I do know how to make johnny-cake," she added, "and gingerbread, and apple pudding. And I can put up preserves, and pickle fish."

"Well, now," said Henry heavily, "that's a good thing. My mother, she never took much to cooking. But you know something? The one thing she liked to make was pickled fish. She said my grandma taught her."

As suddenly as she had turned coy, she turned serious again. "Of course, I can keep house pretty good," she said. "I had to, mostly, after my pa died. It broke my mother's heart, and she took to her bed."

"That's too bad," said Henry. "How did he come to die?"

"He was killed," she said simply. "He was killed at Gettysburg."

The autumn sunlight fell about them, serene and shining. In that clear air, time and the years seemed to stand still, like an azure tide, translucent, full, all motion ended, held for a moment beyond ebb or flow. The sun gleaming, the chipmunk scolding, the twig breaking . . . today or yesterday, yesterday or tomorrow. . . .

What has the spirit to do with tomorrow or yesterday? No more than the sun shining in the sky, no more than the sparrow flirting in the leaves. Earth renews herself, the seasons turn in their long course around the sun, the stars flame far away in the infinite dark; the light falls on Babylon and Rome. It is only a moment between generations, the length of a candle in the wind. And the heart is at home everywhere, in one century as in another.

"He was a soldier," she said. "He fought for the Union. He was brave; and he died."

She sat staring before her, her slender hands clasped in her lap. "It seems like long ago," she said.

He felt a sudden pang of anguish, of jealousy for this man who had loved her, and whom she had loved. She must have known what he was thinking, for she turned, and putting out her hand, touched his arm shyly. "Maybe that's why I like you," she said. "Because you're a soldier, too.

"Even if you didn't fight in the war."

"The war?" said Henry stupidly. "I fought in it, all right. Who said I didn't?"

She was as quick to take offense as he was. "Well, my gracious," she cried, "I didn't know. You don't have to get mad about it. Anyway, the Union soldiers wore blue."

He was silent for a moment, thinking about it. "We fought for the union too," he said at last. "For more than the union. For freedom everywhere; and union everywhere. But what we fought for, and what we'll get . . . Well, I don't know. Anyhow, there wasn't any other choice. You can't have a world half free, and half slaves."

"That's what my father thought," she said.

"I wish I'd known your father," said Henry.

She reached out, and let her hand rest for a moment on his. "I wish you had," she said simply. "Only now you never will."

When he laced his fingers in hers, she made no attempt to draw them away. "Anyhow, I know you," he said. "And that's all I care about."

"Is it, Henry?" she asked steadily.

"Yes," he said.

He took a deep breath. He felt frightened, but

he knew what he had to do; he knew what he wanted to say, and that now was the time when he had to say it. He hoped the words would come out right; he hoped they would mean to her what he wanted them to mean. "There's always something that matters most," he began slowly, "but it takes a long time to get to it. When I was a kid, I thought it was a dog, or a knife. And sometimes I thought it was a girl, or winning a game. And then later it was the war, and staying alive.

"But all the time those things were only a part of it; there was something else, and I missed it. I never did wholly know what it was; but it felt like God.

"Now I know it was you; and that was why it felt like God. Because God is at the end of everything. He has to be; there's nothing beyond Him. If you were to go right out of the world, He's all you'd find. And if you went down deep into your heart, that's where He'd be. Probably you wouldn't ever know Him at all, otherwise.

"When I go into my heart, you're there. And if ever I go out of the world, you'll be there, too. Like God. I don't know how I know it, but I do.

"I'm only thinking things out. I don't know what sense it makes. Don't laugh, anyway."

She turned to him, her eyes dark and wide, her lips parted, and trembling. "I'm not laughing," she said. "I'm nearer crying."

"Well, don't cry, either," he said.

An almost intolerable feeling of sweetness welled up in his breast. His throat ached, and his eyes smarted . . . This was the world, and everything in it, this breathless pause, this single moment: the bud of spring, the rose of summer. This was the answer to death. "Eileen," he whispered.

"Yes," she breathed. She lifted herself against him, she lifted her mouth to him, ineffably soft, infinitely tender. Her lips were full of longing, pity, and delight; the fresh fragrance of her hair enveloped him, along with the clean, hot iron smell of linen, and a faint odor of lavender. Her eyes, so close to his, were like a single pool of darkness; her hands clung to his arms; he thought, with surprise, how strongly she held him. "Yes," she murmured.

She thrust herself out at arm's length, to stare at him hungrily. "Is it really true?" she asked. "Oh, heavens."

"I love you," he said.

"Do you?" she breathed. "It's so . . . so . . . I never thought . . ." And she added, wonderingly, "I love you too, Henry."

He drew her close again; this time she came reluctantly, as though she still wanted to hold herself away, to watch, and savor. "It had to be like this," he murmured fiercely. "It had to be."

"I know," she said. "It's like a book; it's like a wonderful story. Are you sure you love me, Henry? Oh, what will people say? Theodore . . ."

"No," he cried. "Hush, Eileen."

The silence folded over them like the sea; from infinitely far away he heard the crows calling; the sunlight fell upon them from another world. He felt only the soft body in his arms, under the dolman cloak, he remembered only the lifting curve of the throat, the lips parted and subdued, the dark look, half secret, and half shaken. They sat together on the wall, her head against his shoulder, her fingers clasped in his; and the autumn air held them in stillness. Her bonnet had fallen off, it hung from its ribbons around her neck. For a long time, they said nothing.

"Henry," she murmured at last.

"Yes?" His voice was husky, he had difficulty in saying anything.

"We'll have to tell them. You know . . . they all meant me to marry someone else."

He nodded, dumbly. He hadn't been thinking about that. He hadn't been thinking about anything.

"We'll have to tell Theodore," she said. She was still quiet, but practical.

"Poor Theo," she sighed.

"I wish we didn't," he said. "I wish we didn't have to tell anybody. I wish it could just go on, the way it's been. Just between you and me."

"I know," she said. "It's been sweet. But it can't be that way, not any more. Not now. Some day again, maybe, when we can be alone again . . . when we have the right to be. We can't be alone any more now; not till we're married. It wouldn't be safe. It wouldn't be right.

"Will you tell Theo, Henry? I'd rather you did, than me."

"Yes," he said. "I'll tell him."

But it was unnecessary after all; for when he

turned, Theodore was there, within a few feet of them. He had come up unnoticed, and now stood, pale and anguished, leaning against a tree. "You don't need to tell me anything," he said in a trembling voice. "I've seen it all."

He turned away, and started down the sloping path, wiping his eyes with his knuckles. "I won't be around here for long," he said. "No, not for long. "Oh, Jezebel!"

CHAPTER TWELVE

I T was late in the afternoon when Henry got home. Ivy met him at the door — a bleak, grim Ivy, with a pale face and glittering eyes. "You come with me, young man," she said. "It seems to me you've made enough trouble in this house."

She led the way upstairs to Theodore's room. It was the room that Henry knew best of all, for it had been his own; it had been his room ever since he could remember. He looked around him curiously; but there was nothing familiar there any more, it was Theodore's room now. The heavy poster-bed, the large bureau, the maple washstand with the china bowl and pitcher, were all strange; none of the furniture was like what he remembered, nothing was the way it used to be. Even the wall-paper was different. Only the view from the window was the same, looking up the valley, north toward Hemlock.

Theodore was standing in the middle of the room, his hair untidy, his collar awry, his face still streaked with the trace of tears. A small trunk, made of wood, and half packed, stood open before him on the floor.

"There," said Ivy, pointing bitterly to the trunk; "see what you've done. He's leaving me. My son is going away."

"To Ohio," said Theodore.

"That's your doing," said Ivy to Henry. "You've broke his heart."

Lifting his chin, Theodore stared gloomily at the window. "Maybe it's all for the best," he said at last. "Maybe it was meant this way."

"Stuff and nonsense," said Ivy. "It's not for the best at all, nor any part of best. And it wasn't meant, either. God never meant a son to leave his father's home.

"That girl . . ."

She set her lips together in a firm line. "She'd

ought to be tarred and feathered," she declared.

"No, Ma," said Theodore; "don't you go to blame Eileen. She had a right to do what she did." A slight sob escaped him, followed by a hiccup. "Ohio," he said.

"I don't feel very good," said Ivy. "There's pains around my heart. I'll blame who I please."

With an unhappy look, but in a dogged manner, Theodore turned back to the trunk again. "I'll write to you, Ma," he said. "I'll write you a letter."

"That don't suit me at all," declared Ivy. "Wait till your pa hears about this."

He hesitated a moment, holding a suit of under-wear in his hands. "Well," he said finally, with a sort of mild relief, "I won't be here."

"You won't be far either," said Ivy. "Not without money, you won't."

"I've forty dollars saved up," said Theodore. He bent down over the trunk, and laid the underwear away. "She's jilted me," he said.

His voice trembled a little. "Tell John he can have my collection of birds' eggs," he said. "He can have my cow boots, and my fishing pole. I won't need it any more. And he can have my old school-

books, and my glass paperweight with the snow-
fall in it."

A single tear slid down his mother's cheek. She
stood with one hand on her hip, her head bent a
little to one side, like a grieving bird. "I don't aim
to let you go," she said. "Not in this life."

"It would purely kill me."

"There's other girls," said Theodore. "There's
other fish in the sea. I'm going to Dayton, Ohio."

Henry looked at Theodore in surprise. Why, he
thought, he's enjoying this. I could swear he's lay-
ing it on. Maybe he's not as unhappy as he's trying
to give out. "Why Dayton?" he asked.

In reply, he received a swift, and vengeful look.
"I prefer not to talk to you, Mr. Henry Arkbester,"
said Theodore coldly. "If you are an Arkbester," he
added, "which I wouldn't know."

Henry saw his great-grandmother's eyes turn
slowly toward him, cold and reflective, narrow with
dislike. "Hm," she said.

She seemed to come to a decision of some kind.
"You, Henry," she said, "I've got no call to thank
you for what you've done. I guess you won't be
staying here any more, but before you go, there's

one thing more you can do. You can go over to Craik's Farm for me, with a message."

"Craik's Farm?" asked Henry in dismay. No, he thought, I don't want to do that.

Ivy continued: "I want you to take a message from me to Eileen. I want you to tell her that Ivy Arkbester wants to see her. You tell her I want to hear from her own lips whether everything's finished between her and Theodore. Then I'll be satisfied; and not till then."

For a moment, but only a moment, he hesitated. He wanted with all his heart to refuse to go; but somehow, he couldn't say it. There was some quality in her, something indomitable, stubborn, and unforgiving, which was bound to have its way; you could break it, if you were stronger, but it would never let go of itself. He couldn't help respecting it, it was in his blood.

"Yes, ma'am," he said; but his heart was heavy. This is the end of something, he thought; it's never going to be like it was, again.

"It won't do any good for her to come here," said Theodore. "I saw what I saw. I heard her, and him, too."

"That don't impress me," said Ivy. "I know about women, and I know what women want. That Eileen is no fool — even if she is a trifler.

"You go fetch her, young man, and bring her here. Then we'll see what we'll see."

Henry went to the barn, and hitched up the horse and the light buggy. He looked around for the chaplain, for he wanted very much to talk to him; but the chaplain was nowhere in sight. He's off somewhere with Absalom, Henry thought. I guess he can't help me.

The shadows at the end of day covered the fields as he started down the road. The dimness of air, the sadness of earth, seemed like part and picture of his own anxious feelings, his own mournful apprehensions. The sun's almost down, he thought vaguely. The grey is in the air.

It was not only that the bright day was over; it was as if something besides the day were coming to an end, as if something more than the sun were going down. Yet it was only a feeling, he had nothing really to be afraid of. Eileen had promised . . .

Just the same, the private secret between them had lost some of its secret quality. Nothing would ever be quite the same again, probably; they would never be alone again as they had been, cupped in the great, wide hollow of the sky, beyond time and tomorrow . . .

Already in the valley the shadows were deepening, the last green light of day was shining in the west. In the twilit air the well-remembered countryside no longer seemed pleasantly familiar, but gloomy, and forbidding. It's almost as though I didn't belong here, he thought; and he felt a chill at his heart. "Go on," he said to the horse; "hurry."

Evening was falling when he drew up at the Farm. Eileen came out onto the porch to meet him. "Why, Henry," she exclaimed, half delighted, half alarmed, "what are you doing here?"

When he gave her the message Ivy had sent, she grew pale, and bit her lip. "Oh no," she whispered, "I can't."

But they both knew that she would go. She stood frowning, trying to think, her finger at her mouth, her little slipper tapping the floor. "I suppose I have to," she said, after a while. "I wish I didn't. But she'd go to Uncle Cyrus . . .

"Well," she said, taking a deep breath, "I'll get my wrap."

She was out again in a moment, climbing silently onto the seat beside him. He tucked a woolen throw around her knees, and picked up the reins. His hands felt weak where he had touched her knees. "I love you," he said.

She held his hand, tight, for the least part of a second. "Don't you mind, Henry," she said. "It'll be all right."

But there was a lump in his throat. "Sure," he said. "It has to be."

They drove slowly back, up the long valley road, through the blue evening. She sat close to him, without speaking; and Henry felt half fright and half rapture at her nearness, at the knowledge that all her thoughts, her dreams, her hopes were concerned with him; and at that sense of sorrow for which he could find no understandable reason, but which hovered about him, nevertheless, like a mist. He no longer felt secure; it seemed to him that his whole life hung in the balance of this moment, that he himself, his longing, his happiness, and his despair hung upon a single thread, a burden perhaps too heavy for it. A woman's word against the world, a girl's will against the dark. Though why he should be so afraid of Ivy and Theodore, he did not know.

Darkness was beginning; he could hear the night wind rising in the west. The air was colder now, raw and damp, and he bent to tuck the woolen throw more snugly around her. "The wind's coming up," he said; "it'll be a cold night." She nodded her head. "It's been a windy year," she said. "Everybody says it was the windiest year they can remember."

She let her hand slide down between them, next to his; he could feel the warmth of it, and it gave him courage. "Don't let them take you away from me," he said.

Her fingers pressed his bravely. "They won't," she answered; "never fear. How could they?"

"I don't know," he said doubtfully. "Anyway, they'll try."

She was thoughtful for a moment, sitting silent, her hand in his. "I think you'd better stay close beside me, Henry," she said at last. "What we'll do is, we'll go in together. Then I won't mind it so much, seeing them."

"I don't know as they'll let me, Eileen," he said.

"Well," she said, "don't be afraid. Because I'm not. But even if I am, a little . . .

"No," she said firmly; "I'm not.

"And anyway," she said, "how could they take us away from each other? Because I have you in my heart. Forever and ever."

She gave a faint cry. It embarrassed her to have said such a thing; but it had come out before she knew it. She blushed, and looked away, pressing the back of her hand to her mouth, and holding her breath for fear of what he might think of her. But it only seemed to make him happy.

"Forever and ever," he said. "No matter what?"

She turned and looked at him, her cheeks still pink but her gaze level and unflinching.

"No matter what," she said.

CHAPTER THIRTEEN

HENRY was right: Ivy had no intention of letting him be present at her talk with Eileen. She barred the way . . . first leading Eileen into the parlor, and then placing herself between them in the doorway, her hand on her hip, and her head to one side, the way she had. "Yes?" she said; "were you aiming to go anywheres?"

"Why," said Henry, "I think I ought to be along in there with you, when you talk."

Ivy nodded bleakly. "You do," she declared. "Well, I don't."

He looked at her in silence; he could feel the heat in back of his eyes. "Well," he said, "we sort of think I ought to. Eileen, too."

"I don't much care," she said. "It's my house, and

I figure to arrange things to suit myself. You had things your own way; and now it's my turn." She bent her head around to glance at the girl behind her. "It's time you and me had a little understanding," she said. She was not unfriendly about it; her voice was tired, but firm; and she sighed. "I don't feel very good," she said. "I don't feel like arguing."

Eileen gave her a quick, frightened smile. "Yes, ma'am," she said. "I know. Only . . ."

"What I've got to say," declared Ivy, "don't concern anyone but you and me. When I've said it, you can do as you please."

"Well," said Eileen slowly; "well . . ." She seemed to give in all at once. "All right, then," she said. She drew her breath in, quick and unsteady. "Wait for me, Henry," she said. "Don't go away."

The last thing he saw was her white face and her dark eyes staring at him, as the door closed. He stood leaning against it, feeling afraid, and weak; he clenched his fists in front of him, and looked down at them unhappily. "Oh golly," he whispered. It was what he used to say when he was a boy.

He felt very young — strangely young — and helpless. It seemed like so much more than a wooden door, somehow, between himself and Eileen; it was not at all as though she were in the next room, only a few feet away, and he were there, waiting outside. It was more than that, and farther away; it was more like darkness and a wind between them, and distance out of sight and cry. It was as though where she was, was life; and where he was waiting, was somewhere else, the other side of the night, perhaps . . . the other side of the sky.

Sick with sadness, he leaned his head against the cold wood of the door, which was so frail, and which he was so powerless to open. "Oh darling," he whispered. "Don't let them do anything to us."

He could hear them speaking inside; he listened for her voice. But it was Ivy who was doing all the talking; he could hear her level tones, sharp and dry, bitter as old tea. It was she who asked the questions, and answered them herself.

"And so," she was saying (and he realized with a sudden wave of anxiety that he had missed whatever had been said before), "he didn't tell you who he was, after all? Now, that's purely trifling of him. I know he says his name is Arkbester — Henry Arkbester, he calls himself; but who's that? Let me tell you something; we never heard of anybody by the name of Henry Arkbester, Mr. Arkbester and me. There's been no Henry in the family for nigh on to fifty years; and as for his parents, I never heard of them, neither."

He could hear Eileen draw in her breath, in a little gasp. "It isn't true," she said. But there was no strength in her voice.

"Well, it is," said Ivy patiently. "I'm not lying to you. We don't know anything about him, who he is, or where he comes from. If you know, then you tell me; where'd he come from? Maybe he told you."

"No," said Eileen, after a while; "he didn't tell me."

"There you are, then," said Ivy. "I'm going to put the sheriff on him."

"He told me," said Eileen, ". . . he told me . . ." Her voice wavered with fright and defiance. "He told me he was going to own this house some day."

The silence which followed this announcement was tense with unbelief, with outrage, and with scorn. Henry could almost see Ivy's face, hard as

stone, and the way she must have stood there looking at her, her eyes half closed, thinking and planning. "He did, did he?" she said heavily at last.
"Well, well.

"Well, he isn't," she said. "I can promise you
that."

She seemed to take a few steps around the room.
"No," she said quietly after a while; "it's Theodore's
house when I'm gone. And that's not likely to be
long now, I feel that poorly. I haven't much further
to go along my way. I aim to leave the house to
Theodore and his wife; I always figured to do that.
There's some fixing to be done first; we figure to
put a porch on the south side, off the parlor. A
porch is nice for sitting, in summer.

"Yes," she went on thoughtfully, and her voice
was slow and full of meaning, "a nice, sitting porch.
And Theodore, he has his heart set on one of those
new-fangled marble wash-stands from Philadelphia. Well, I say he can have it, time he gets married. Of course, there's my sewing machine; I
wouldn't want to leave that to Becky, she's too
young for it.

"I suppose Theodore'll have a tidy little sum of money some day. Between what I've got to leave him, and his pa."

It seemed to Henry that Eileen's answer was a long time coming. And as the pause grew and deepened, a terrible fear began to take hold of him. Why wasn't she talking back? Why didn't she say the things she'd promised? It was as though some slow, dreadful change were taking place there on the other side of the door, a change like the change in a dream, where the unexpected disaster looms up suddenly without warning, a chill, a shadow in the bright sky . . . some break-down of goodness, and the panic-feeling turning his bones to water as he stood there, rooted to the ground (and that, too, how like a dream) — helpless to move, to stop the evil thing that was happening, helpless even to cry out, except for one hoarse croak, "Eileen."

And on the other side of the door, Ivy's voice went on, firm with triumph:

"The country's full of young women who have left a good home and family to follow some smooth-voiced stranger, and end their days in shame and disgrace. You think it over, Eileen. You're a sensible young woman. A nice home, a decent, God-fearing husband . . ."

Leaning there against the cold woodwork of the door, he closed his eyes. And in his mind, he saw Eileen before him; and it seemed to him that she was waiting for him to speak. What have you got to say to me, Henry? she asked. What have you got to give me?

Still with his eyes closed, he shook his head in anguish. What had he to give her, compared to Ivy? A house, a porch, a sewing machine? No — they were Ivy's, and after Ivy, Theodore's. This was Ivy's home, not his; this was long ago.

"When I go into my heart, you're there. And if ever I go out of the world, you'll be there, too. I don't know how I know it, but I do."

That was what he had to give her . . . only the heart's long hunger, the endless, shadowy longing. That was all that he had to offer her. Only that; nothing more.

So there it was. He didn't even want to wait to hear her answer. Because whatever it might be, he knew that it couldn't change anything. "Don't say it," he told her in his mind; "not yet, not now. I know what you want to tell her; and that's true. But what Ivy says is true, too. I'm only a homeless stranger here. I'm only something in your heart, and you in mine. Not here; not now."

As he turned slowly away, he met Absalom in the hall, coming in. "Now, then, young man," said Absalom heartily, "what's going on in here? Where's Ivy? Where's my supper?"

Henry motioned with his thumb at the closed door of the parlor. "She's in there," he said.

The tone of his voice took Absalom by surprise. "What's the matter?" he asked sharply. "You been took sick?"

"No, sir," said Henry. "I'm all right."

"Well, by God," said Absalom, "you look sick as a cow to me. You look like you were just about griped to death. What's she doing in the parlor, this time of night?"

Henry shook his head dumbly. "She's just talking," he said.

"Talking? What about? Don't the woman know I want my supper?"

He strode heavily toward the parlor; but he never got there. For at that moment, John came tearing in from the kitchen. He was out of breath; and his eyes were popping half out of his head with horror and delight. "Oh Pa," he gasped when he saw Absalom; "Oh Pa."

Absalom wheeled, and caught him by the shoulder. "What is it, boy?" he cried. "What's got in you? Tearing in here like the place was on fire . . ."

Spun about by the impact of his father's hand, John stood there, shaking, taking in great gulps of air, trying to get his breath. "It's Becky," he got out at last. "She's gone."

Absalom shook him till his teeth rattled. "What do you mean, gone," he roared; "gone where? Speak up, speak up; don't stand there like a nincompoop. Where's she gone to?"

Whatever joy John had felt as bearer of the bad news, ran out of him like water out of a drain. He looked at his father's blazing face, and burst into tears. "I tell you she's gone," he sobbed. "She's run away. She's run away with the goods peddler."

CHAPTER FOURTEEN

John's tears did not last very long; they were soon dried, and sniffled back into his nose. He had a story to tell, and he set himself to tell it, in a meaty way. It seemed to him that it was like a story in a book, full of savory wonder.

"I thought they was up to something," he said, "the way they kept meeting down by the school-house. I tried to tell you, Pa, but you shushed me up. You and Ma; remember? You said you didn't want to hear no more about it, and Ma said she was too pure-minded, and stuff like that."

"Where are they?" cried Absalom. "That's all I want to know."

"I don't know where they are," said John, "but I know where they're heading. I thought there was something funny, the way she was in her room with the door locked all afternoon. So I looked in, first chance I got, and there was her old satchel, the one she got for Christmas that time, packed up with all her clothes in it. So I just naturally sort of waited to see."

"Don't irritate me, boy," said Absalom. "Just tell me where they're heading."

But John had to tell it his own way. "So first thing I see," he went on stubbornly, "is Becky coming out of the house looking scared as a rabbit, and carrying her satchel like she didn't want anybody to see her. She didn't notice me, on account of I was hid in a place I know. So pretty soon, along comes this goods peddler, and they run off together, with him toting the satchel."

"By God," cried Absalom, reaching for him, "you tell me where they've gone before I peel the hide off you."

"Yes sir," said John. "I was going to tell you. They're heading for Philadelphia. I heard them say so. Only they got to go down the road a ways first, to where he left his wagon."

Absalom looked wildly around him. "Philadelphia, hey?" he said. "Then they got to go up through the ravine. Where's my gun?"

"It's hanging on the wall, Pa," said John. And he added happily,

"Can I go with you? Can I, Pa?"

But his moment of glory was over. He was thrown aside as Absalom strode to the parlor door, and flung it open. He stood on the threshold like a figure of doom, his very beard quivering with wrath as he faced his wife. "You, Ivy," he said; "while you been gossiping and palavering, your daughter's run off with a traveling peddler. I'm going after her. You take yourself into the kitchen, and get me my supper for when I get back."

Without another word, he turned and made for the office where he kept his gun. But Henry stood where he was, looking in at the two women in the parlor. He seemed to see them from some place far away, as though he no longer belonged to their world, or they to his. They were like dolls, with small, blank faces and tiny, surprised gestures; they were like people at the wrong end of a telescope, transported suddenly into a different dimension, made lilliputian and unreal. He heard Ivy give a faint cry, he saw her put her hand to her heart, and fall slowly sideways to the floor; and he thought, she's got it now, after all her talk. He saw Eileen's pale, horror-struck face staring at him across the prostrate body of his great-grandmother; and he thought, now the way is clear for you. He had no feeling of bitterness, only a great weariness. I don't know what got into us, he thought, or why it was like it was. Nothing was ever so beautiful before. . . . It was as if it had to be; and all the time, it couldn't be, only we didn't know it. It wasn't anybody's fault; not yours, Eileen, or mine. I guess we always loved each other; I guess we always will. But always is forever, and life is only a little while.

They did not speak to each other; they had nothing to say. They looked at each other in silence, across an endless space, across a bridge of memory frailer than air. The infinite distances of time widened between them, quieter than stillness, deeper than pain. "My love," he said; "Eileen."

Then he turned and went away. He had still one last thing to do.

He found the chaplain waiting for him outside the kitchen door. "We have to hurry," he said.

They struck out together across the wet fields, back along the way they had come that first day. It was dark; clouds covered the sky, and the wind was blowing steady and cold. Henry could hear it singing stronger and stronger in the air above him. "I'm surely sorry to have brought you into all this," he said apologetically, "but I didn't know. I thought I was just coming home, like any other time."

The chaplain did not seem at all put out, or in any way surprised. He strode along beside Henry, and his face reflected only a gentle friendliness. "What puzzles me," said Henry, "is how it was all different from what I thought. I used to think folks must have known what they wanted . . . I guess I thought that things were simpler in the old days, and people were better. I figured that God was closer, then; but now I don't think so."

"God has never been any closer to the world," replied the chaplain, "or any further away from it."

"Still," said Henry thoughtfully, "when we pray, He seems nearer."

"Those who pray," agreed the chaplain, "draw near, through innocence and humility. But those who ask favors for themselves, receive an inscrutable reply."

"I only asked for love," said Henry. The chaplain nodded his head.

"That is what I mean," he said.

By now they had entered the woods, and had begun the long climb toward Bitter's Ravine. It was too dark to see, but Henry walked swiftly, as though he knew the way. I've got to warn Becky, he thought; I've got to keep Absalom from doing the thing that's in his mind. He wondered for a moment why he should be the one who had to do this; why he cared so much, why it was so important for him to get there in time. It wasn't for Becky's sake, he knew — as much as he liked her; or for Absalom, either. When the answer came to him, he knew that it was right, because it made everything clear and simple. It was for Eileen's sake that he had to get there, and keep Absalom from harming anyone. She'd never be happy if there was trouble, he told himself. She'd never take pleasure in all those pretty things she wanted. She'd never take pleasure in anything again.

He thought he heard her voice, far off and faint, and a little out of tune. "And if I should never see him again, it will break my heart, or nearly."

"I don't want your heart to be broke," he told her. "Not any more than a little bit."

"Because you are in my heart," she whispered, "Forever and ever."

"That's why," he told her.

He thought of the peddler, and he smiled in the darkness. "He tried to sell me stock in the Santa Fe Railroad," he said to the chaplain. "He believed in the future, but he didn't believe enough. It would have seemed wonderful to him, if he could have seen it."

"Do you believe in the future?" asked the chaplain.

"I don't know," said Henry.

It seemed to Henry that the chaplain sighed faintly. "Still," he said, "you believe in the past."

"I know where I've been," said Henry. "But that don't say I know where I'm going."

"You have been at home," said the chaplain, "and you have seen the beginning of an age of wonders. Yet, where you came from, in your own time, that age was already in full flower, and the wonders were old. Where you are going, I cannot tell you, for it is a mystery, even to me. But I can tell you this much: beyond the world you have seen, lies the world of the spirit; and it, too, is full of marvels. Men have learned to use air and earth and all metals; to fly above the clouds, and talk to each other across the seas. But they have not learned to use the power of love; they have not learned to use the power in their own hearts. They have not yet glimpsed the marvels which lie ahead of them."

"And is that," asked Henry, "where God is?"

The chaplain was silent. "I cannot tell you," he said at last, simply. "I do not know."

The path grew steeper in the darkness, but still Henry hurried on, between the trees. He knew the path so well . . . his childhood walked with him, and kept him company. He thought of his mother and his father, he thought of his boyhood, of his early hopes and later plans, of how he had wanted to grow up in the world, to be an important man — a flyer, perhaps, or a radio engineer . . . He thought of Eileen. He tried to imagine her there in the darkness beside him, the way he had before; but Theodore's face kept coming between them. What was the good of it all, he wondered; what had his life amounted to? "I haven't done anything I wanted," he said. "I haven't had anything."

He heard the chaplain's voice behind him: "It is not what you had, but what you were, my son. Love brought you into the world, even though you had little for yourself. Yet love is not a gift, it is not a reward for anything. It is like the sea from which our life first came. It is the cradle of us all."

"You, too?" asked Henry.

"Yes," said the chaplain.

Henry stepped briskly along the path. "It's funny how they thought the South would always be bitter," he said. "I guess they didn't know."

"Bitterness brings nothing into the world," declared the chaplain; "and it does not last very long."

"I didn't last very long, either," said Henry.

"Long enough," said the chaplain. "You had little; but what you had, you gave."

A feeling of peace and pride flowed through Henry Arkbester's heart. "Well, thanks," he said. "Thank you, sir."

But somewhere on ahead was Absalom with the old fowling piece, and murder in his mind; and somewhere behind them, on another road headed up through the pass, were Becky and Mr. Neuberger. Henry felt sorry for Becky. "You didn't turn out the way they thought," he said to her, as though she were there; "you wanted to live in a big city, and wear nice clothes. But all your mother wanted for you was to be pure. She cared a lot for purity, your mother did; she liked it more than kindness, even. I don't know can you be pure without being kind. Not in the good sense of the words. Now, you take us, you take the fellows and the girls I knew back home: we didn't think much of purity, we thought of freedom. I guess you can't be free either, without you've got kindness for others."

He thought he felt the chaplain's hand for a moment, like a benediction, on his shoulder. Then it was gone; and turning, he found himself alone. "Are you there, sir?" he cried into the darkness; but there was no answer. He's gone, he thought; I've lost him. I'll have to do this by myself, now.

The wind was blowing harder, he could feel the

tug and push of it even down there among the trees. A slant of rain caught him in the face, like a little shower of ice water. He could hear the tree-tops creak, and the branches sough and rustle all around him. "You, Absalom," he cried; "where are you?"

There was no answer. He thought that he caught a glimpse of a dark shape on the path ahead of him, but the night came down in a curtain of rain around him, and he lost sight of it again. He hurried on, buffeted by the wind, slipping a little on the roots and stones. . . . He knew that he must be near the road now, where it came up through the pass. That was where Absalom would be, he thought — waiting.

He came through the wet trees by the low stone wall, and saw the road before him, a grey patch in the night. He peered about him, but in the darkness trees and bushes merged into a single shadow. If Absalom was there, he was keeping himself hidden. He spoke into the blackness, with desperate urgency.

"Absalom," he said, "if you're there — listen. Children don't always know what's good for them;

they have to be told. But who's to tell them so they'll understand? The old can't tell the young anything; not that they'll listen to. Let them be, and forgive them."

The rain whispered, and the wind soughed; and that was all. And then, all at once, faintly from down the road, he heard the creak of wheels and the hollow sound of a horse's hoofs. A lantern appeared suddenly from around a curve, star-bright and far away, disappeared behind a clump of trees, and emerged again a little nearer. He could see the vague loom of the wagon, and the lantern light glinting on the wheels, sliding like a yellow lozenge over the ground.

And at the same time, close at hand, he saw the dark shadow that was Absalom disengage itself from the darker mass of trees and bushes by the roadside, and move silently out into the middle of the road. Well, he thought, this is it.

He felt clear and happy; he knew that he had got there in time. With all his might, he shouted to Mr. Neuberger to jump from the wagon and run. Then he launched himself through the darkness.

He saw Absalom swing around toward him, startled, with the gun pointing at his breast. He did not hear the gun go off. But the last thing he saw, was light.

CHAPTER FIFTEEN

Up on Hemlock Mountain, above Millersville and Landons, the sheriff and his men were searching the wreckage of the plane which had crashed and burned near Bitter's Ravine. The wind was still blowing steady and cold, but the clouds had lifted; the storm had gone off into the east, and in a little while the sun would be up. A few farmers and most of the boys of the region had gathered at the wreck, and stood about in awkward, unhappy groups at the edge of the charred ground. Young Jimmy Leadbetter, whose family raised corn and peas on what used to be Craik's Farm, and Oscar Pfeifer, whose father ran the radio and bicycle shop in Millersville, gazed at the scene with reverent and speculative eyes. "She was a big one," said

Jimmy; "and when she hit . . . kerblam."

"She was a transcontinental," said Oscar, "heading for Philadelphia. She must have been off her course by ten, twelve miles."

"O boy," said Jimmy; "there was a lot killed."

"Most twenty-five," said Oscar. "All of them," he added, with somber relish.

"They didn't get no chance at all," said Jimmy. "They must have died smacko."

All at once tears of inexplicable grief welled up in his eyes, and rolled down his cheeks. He gave a single sniffle, and wiped his nose with the back of his hand. "Jeez," he observed, "it don't smell good."

Oscar cast a reflective eye over the ground. "You see those blackberry bushes?" he asked. "Well, come summer, you wouldn't know there'd been a fire here at all."

He dropped his voice a little; he spoke out of the side of his mouth. "We could build a house out of that stuff the wings was made of," he said, "if they was to leave it."

"Well, we could, all right," said Jimmy.

He saw the house in imagination, of shining metal, a little rusted in spots, but firm and water-tight. "We could build a swell house," he said.

Farther out on the charred ground, but still a little distance from the plane, two men were bending over the body of a soldier. The flames had missed him, except for a small burned patch in his tunic, near the heart. One of the men picked up a square, leather portfolio which had fallen, half open, from the soldier's pocket, and glanced at it curiously. Then he showed it to his companion.

"Look," he said. "This here must have been his girl."

They stared at the faded picture together, at the girl's face which peered out at them over the signature: "To Henry, with all my love, Eileen." Then they looked down in silence at the dead man. He lay on his back, his face calm and peaceful, lighted by the rising sun.

"He went quick and sudden when he went," one of them said. "It must have got him before he knew it."

He shook his head in mild wonder. "Looks like his last thoughts was good ones," he said.